SHERRYL WOODS

ONE TOUCH OF MOONDUST

SILHOUETTE *Desire*

Published by Silhouette Books New York

America's Publisher of Contemporary Romance

SILHOUETTE BOOKS
300 East 42nd St., New York, N.Y. 10017

ISBN: 0-373-05521-8

First Silhouette Books printing September 1989

Bold Blue Eyes Examined Her With Leisurely Thoroughness.

As if on cue, impudent lips emitted an approving whistle. Light brown hair waved in casual and charming disarray. Faded, paint-spattered jeans clung to narrow hips and muscular thighs.

Despite the chill in the air, a shirt hung open, revealing a chest covered with coarse brown hair that arrowed provocatively downward.

Gabrielle was torn between clutching her coat more protectively around her and stripping it away from her suddenly burning flesh.

She settled for trying to stare him down.

The attempt failed miserably.

He laughed, an all-too-knowing gleam in his eyes. "So what's a sophisticated lady like you doing in a place like this? Slumming?"

Dear Reader:

As you can see, Silhouette Desire has a bold new cover design that we're all excited about. But while the overall look is new, two things remain the same. First, we've kept our eye-catching red border. You can be sure to always spot Silhouette Desires on the shelves! Second, between these new covers are the high-quality love stories that you've come to expect.

In addition, the MAN OF THE MONTH program continues with Mr. September, who comes from the pen of Dixie Browning. Clement Cornelius Barto is a unique hero who is sure to charm you with his unusual ways. But make no mistake, it's not just *Beginner's Luck* that makes him such a winner.

October brings you a man who's double the fun, because not only is Jody Branigan an exciting hero, he's also one of Leslie Davis Guccione's Branigan brothers. Look for his story in *Branigan's Touch*.

We at Silhouette have been happy to hear how much you've all enjoyed the Year of the Man. The responses we've received about the special covers— and to each and every one of our heroes—has been enthusiastic. Remember, there are more men ahead in 1989—don't let any of them get away!

Yours,

Lucia Macro
Senior Editor

Books by Sherryl Woods

Silhouette Desire

Not at Eight, Darling #309
Yesterday's Love #329
Come Fly with Me #345
A Gift of Love #375
Can't Say No #431
Heartland #472
One Touch of Moondust #521

Silhouette Special Edition

Safe Harbor #425
Never Let Go #446
Edge of Forever #484
In Too Deep #522

SHERRYL WOODS

lives by the ocean, which, she says, provides daily inspiration for the romance in her soul. She further explains that her years as a television critic taught her about steamy plots and humor, her years as a travel editor took her to exotic locations and her years as a crummy weekend tennis player taught her to stick with what she enjoyed most—writing. "What better way is there," Sherryl asks, "to combine all that experience than by creating romantic stories?"

For Lucia Macro,
who sees beyond my blind spots
and always finds the heart of the story,
with thanks for her editing skill,
her patience and her humor.

One

Gabrielle came to a halt in the middle of a cracked sidewalk richly decorated with dramatic and color-fully executed graffiti. She checked the address she'd marked in the paper against two numbers that dan-gled precariously upside down beside a dilapidated building's front door. If the empty space between them had once been filled by a seven, then this was in fact "Recently Renovated Brownstone." Apparently the renovations were less recent than hoped for.

Tucking her chilled hands in the pockets of her coat for warmth, she regarded the faded facade, dirt-streaked bay windows and dingy, peeling trim with a sense of resignation. It was a very long way from Park Avenue. Taking a deep breath of the brisk fall air, she wrapped her fur coat more tightly around her and stepped into the dreary foyer.

It had possibilities, she decided, viewing the muddy tile floor and dull brass fixtures with a critical eye. The construction looked sound enough and she'd be willing to bet that the apartments all had hardwood floors. She seemed to recall a chimney on the outside, which meant there were fireplaces. Yes, it definitely had possibilities, she thought with a vague sense of anticipation, the first she'd felt in weeks.

In fact, a few months earlier when her career on Wall Street had been ascending at a dizzying pace, she might very well have bought the whole place and restored it as a promising investment. Now, with no brokerage house work to be found for a talented but still very junior financial analyst, she could barely afford the advertised bargain rent. In fact, if she didn't make some career decisions soon and find another job, she'd be forced to retreat to her family home in South Carolina and live on humble pie for the rest of her life. It was not an alternative she cared to endure.

Gritting her teeth with determination, she began climbing the endless, creaking steps to apartment 4B, where the smell of fresh paint was wafting through the open door. She considered that an encouraging sign after the dinginess and disrepair below.

Gabrielle tapped on the door and waited. The hammering sounds coming from deep inside the apartment didn't let up. She knocked harder and called out. The pounding stopped.

"Yo," a husky masculine voice responded cheerfully. "Be right with you, sweetheart."

Sweetheart? Gabrielle's vivid imagination immediately supplied an image to go with that impertinent voice: a well-muscled, catcalling construction worker atop steel beams overlooking Fifth Avenue. He'd be rugged, impervious to slights and persistent. She'd walked past the type half a dozen times a day and they'd always made her want to check to see if her slip was showing. When this man emerged a moment later she was startled to see how accurately he fit the image. She was also startled to discover that in this case her slip was the last thing on her mind. The man quite simply took her breath away.

Bold blue eyes examined her with a disconcerting, leisurely thoroughness. As if on cue, impudent lips emitted an approving whistle. Light brown hair, still streaked with highlights from the summer sun, waved in casual and charming disarray. Faded, paint-spattered jeans clung to narrow hips and muscular thighs. Despite the chill in the air, a shirt hung open, revealing a chest covered with coarse brown hair that arrowed provocatively downward. Gabrielle was torn between clutching her coat more protectively around her and stripping it away from her suddenly burning flesh. She settled for trying to stare him down.

The attempt failed miserably. He laughed, an all-too-knowing gleam in his eyes.

"So," he said, amusement lacing through his voice, "what's a sophisticated lady like you doing in a place like this? Slumming?"

Detecting sarcasm rather than humor in the remark, she had to bite back an instinctive angry retort.
He had an apartment. She needed one. It was no time
to look around with the hauteur of Bette Davis and
declare, "What a dump," much less deliver a lecture on
manners to the hired help.

She held up the paper instead. "I've come about the
apartment. May I see it?"

With a wide smile punctuated by dimples, he gave a
grand, sweeping gesture. "Be my guest."

Gabrielle stepped cautiously inside and took a slow
survey of the empty room. She had difficulty register-
ing the apartment's features because the man stood
right behind her, watching her every move. Where she
went, he followed, first with his eyes, then by ambling
along behind. Since he couldn't possibly be concerned
about theft, she had to assume he was doing it to rattle
her.

It was working. Quite well, in fact. She tried to shake
off the feeling with common sense. With her whole life
off-kilter, the last thing she needed was an instanta-
neous physical attraction to a man of apparently limited means and ambition. A handyman, for heaven's
sake. The members of the Junior League of Charleston would die laughing at the notion of Senator Graham Clayton's daughter having palpitations over a
handyman.

"Do you know anything about the building?" she
asked when she'd seen the living room and two tiny
bedrooms. She'd been right about the fireplace. It was
small, but suggestive of cozy winter evenings. She was

less hopeful about the floor. It was wood all right, but paint-spattered, scuffed and marred by several generations of spills. It would require extensive elbow grease, sanding and quite possibly a miracle to restore it.

"What did you want to know about the building?"

"When was the last time an exterminator was here?"

He shrugged doubtfully. "There's always a can of Raid."

One blond brow arched significantly. "I see." She glanced once more around the empty living room. "The ad said furnished."

"It will be."

"When?"

"Tomorrow. Maybe the next day. Whenever I get finished with the work."

The man obviously had a careless disregard for timetables. To a woman whose calendar had always been carefully scheduled in fifteen-minute increments such a blasé attitude was both irritating and irresponsible. "When exactly will it be available?" she persisted. "I'm facing a deadline."

"An anxious client?"

She stared at him blankly. "Client?"

"You're a real estate agent, right? If you want to buy, it's not for sale. If you have someone who wants to rent, I'd prefer to deal direct. Sorry, no agents."

"I'm not in real estate. I'm looking for myself. To rent," she amended, in case he was worried that she was planning to buy the property and fire the help— starting with him.

Instead of putting his mind at ease, though, she seemed to have astonished him. "You actually want to live here yourself?"

"Why not?" she said defensively, though she knew perfectly well what he meant. "It's an apartment. I need a place to live."

"Try Park Avenue."

"I did," she admitted ruefully. "The price is right here."

"So," he said, conducting a more thoughtful survey, "the lady's down on her luck." There was little sympathy in his voice, only mild curiosity.

She drew herself up with dignity and tried to wilt him with a haughty stare. "Temporarily."

The stare had no discernible effect. "Does that mean you'll be moving out the minute you get a few bucks together?"

She considered lying, but figured he'd never believe her if she did. There was a disconcertingly astute gleam in his eyes—one that was all too typical of corporate sharks.

"Yes," she said finally.

"Then why would I want to rent to you?"

"I'm here. I've got the money." At least for the first month, she amended to herself.

"This is New York, sweetheart. You're not the first person to stop by and you won't be the last."

"Are you holding out for the highest bidder?"

"Maybe. What're you offering?"

The speculative look in his eyes brought a flush to Gabrielle's normally pale complexion. This time she did settle her coat more protectively around her and headed for the door. In the past few months she'd sacrificed just about everything but her pride and her dignity. She wasn't about to lose those, as well.

"Never mind," she said on her way out. "I don't think this would work out."

He caught up with her before she could reach the door. "I'm sorry," he said with what sounded like total sincerity. She studied his expression, assessing him as she might a prospective investor. His eyes, for once, were serious, which did the strangest things to her ability to breathe. He touched her sleeve. "Please. Accept my apology. If you want the place, it's yours."

"Why?"

"I've been through a few rough times myself."

The suddenly sympathetic, contrite demeanor made her extraordinarily suspicious. Leopards rarely changed their spots in the blink of an eye. This leopard was also shifting his weight uneasily from one foot to the other. She waited for his next move.

"There is one thing you should know about first, though," he said finally.

"Which is?"

"The bathroom."

Despite herself, she grinned at his cautious tone. "I'm familiar with the concept. I assume this one has all the usual amenities."

"More or less," he said, intriguing her as he beckoned and headed toward the opposite end of the living room. "Through here."

She walked into a narrow kitchen with peeling wallpaper and yellowed linoleum and came to a halt, her mouth dropping open. "I hope that's a planter," she murmured, staring at the large, claw-footed ceramic tub in the middle of the room, then at her guide. He was laughing.

"Nope. That's the tub all right. It's more convenient to the stove in here."

"The stove?" she repeated weakly.

"In case the hot water runs out and you . . ."

"I get the picture. Where's the rest of it?"

"It?"

"The bathroom."

"Through that door."

Deciding it wouldn't be wise to take anything else for granted, Gabrielle peeked through the door. Thankfully there were no more surprises. The sink and toilet appeared old, but functional—she checked just to be sure—and the room was clean.

Now she was the one hesitating. She had finally accepted the idea that her current budget wouldn't allow for luxuries, but a tub in the kitchen? Still, she thought of the long list of depressing, unsatisfactory apartments she'd already seen. With all its flaws—and she wasn't minimizing them—this was still far and away the best.

"Okay," she said eventually, if reluctantly. "I can live with this."

"There's one other thing."

She felt her heart sink. The way he'd said that told her it was even more ominous than having to take her bath in the middle of her kitchen. "What?" she said with a weary sigh.

"If you're in a hurry to move in, you might have to deal with a roommate."

Her eyebrows shot up. She gave him a hard stare. He looked decidedly uneasy again, which was unnerving in a man of his apparent self-confidence. "A roommate? You mean it's already rented?" She felt oddly disappointed.

"Not exactly."

"Well, it's either rented or it's not."

"Actually it's just temporarily occupied."

"Does this have anything to do with the sleeping bag I saw rolled up in one of the bedroom closets?"

He nodded. "It's mine."

That was definitely a problem. "When will you be moving out?"

"In a couple of months, as soon as I can get the apartments downstairs finished, but it's okay. We could share the place until then. It has two bedrooms and I'd promise to stay in mine."

He crossed his heart dramatically, then treated her to that wide, high-voltage smile. Obviously he meant it to be friendly and reassuring. He had no idea that it set her pulse to racing in a way that normally indicated such crises as imminent stock market crashes or a dramatic fall in the value of the dollar. If there had been a chair in the room, she would have collapsed into it. She refused to sit in the tub.

"This isn't such a good idea," she said. It was an eloquent understatement. It was a horrible, impossible, not-to-be-considered-for-an-instant idea. "I'll have to keep looking."

"Where will you go?"

"I don't know. Someplace."

"Can you stay where you are?"

"Not after Saturday."

"Is there a friend you can move in with?"

She thought of several who'd offered, all of them part of the fast-paced, well-heeled world she was leaving behind. "No."

"Can you afford a hotel?"

For the first time she heard a note of compassion in his voice. She sighed. "No."

"Then think about my offer. Come see the garden before you decide," he encouraged, holding out his hand. Gabrielle ignored it and he jammed it into his pocket. The snub didn't faze his upbeat mood as he enthused, "It's a little ragged now, but in the spring with tulips and crocuses and forsythia in bloom, it'll be magnificent. At least that's what my father says and he's got a green thumb that's known all over Long Island."

Gabrielle felt a ridiculous twinge of doubt. She was a sucker for a garden. Always had been. The Clayton house in South Carolina had been surrounded by azaleas and roses with an extravagantly colorful and overgrown English country garden in back that had been her personal domain.

"I'll take a look," she said finally. "But I don't think it will change my mind. I've never had a roommate, not even in college."

Left unspoken was the fact that she'd never lived with a man under any circumstances. Where she came from it still wasn't considered proper, especially for the daughter of a highly recognizable politician. Goodness knows, her relationship with her former fiancé had been proper. Which, she admitted ruefully, was probably part of the problem. With Townsend Lane she hadn't even been tempted to commit a casual indiscretion, much less have a sizzling affair.

She followed her prospective roommate downstairs, through a narrow hallway and onto a tiny stoop. What she saw made her smile in a way that she hadn't smiled in a very long time. A bit of sunshine stole into her heart.

The tiny, walled-in area had flower beds along the fringes. Now they were jammed with a haphazard display of chrysanthemums, marigolds and zinnias in yellows and oranges and reds. A wrought-iron table and two chairs fit tidily into the middle. The whole garden was shaded by a huge maple tree next door, its leaves already turning to the fiery shades of autumn. It was charming, utterly and irresistibly charming.

"What's the rent?" she asked finally. Perhaps if she concentrated on the business aspects of the transaction, she wouldn't be quite so vibrantly aware of the fact that she was committing herself to living with a man she'd met less than an hour earlier. It would be a practical decision under the circumstances, a way to stretch her remaining savings. She waited for his response to see just how far she could make those last dollars go.

"We can work it out."

"Will I have to sign a lease?"

"What for?" he asked. "You've already told me you have every intention of breaking it."

It was an unexpected plus. There would be no arguments when the time came for her to move back out.

"And we're strictly roommates? You have your own room. I have mine. We share the kitchen. Right?" An image of the tub popped into mind. "We have a schedule for the kitchen," she amended.

Apparently the same provocative image lurked in his mind, too, because he grinned. "If you say so."

She took another look around the garden, then held out her hand. "Then I guess we understand each other Mr....?"

He enfolded her hand in his much larger one and held it just long enough for the calluses and warmth to register against the chilled softness of her own flesh.

"Reed," he said in a slow, deliberately provocative way meant to emblazon the name on her memory. "Paul Reed."

She swallowed hard. "And I'm Gabrielle Clayton." It came out sounding disgustingly breathless.

"Gabrielle, huh? Quite a mouthful for such a little bit of a thing. Why don't I call you Gaby?"

She felt her control slipping away and inserted the haughty edge back into her voice. "Gabrielle will do just fine. Ms. Clayton would be even better."

"So, Gaby, when do you want to move in?"

She gave him an icy stare. It was going to be a very long month. Or two. "As soon as possible."

"Will Friday be okay? I should be able to get the basics taken care of by then."

She supposed if she was about to walk straight into danger, it was better to get it over with. "Perfect," she said without the slightest tremor.

"One last thing," she said as she went to the foyer. "For as long as we're sharing the place, we split the rent fifty-fifty."

"That's really not fair. I'm inconveniencing you. I'll take care of the first month. After that you pay the full rate."

She toyed with the temptation, then dismissed it. Being in this man's debt could lead to all sorts of potentially explosive misunderstandings. "Fifty-fifty."

He shrugged. "If that's what you want."

"And the same with the utilities."

"Okay."

"And you call me Gabrielle."

He grinned. "We'll have to work on that one."

He followed her onto the front stoop and watched as she started down the steps. She felt his gaze burning into her.

"Have a nice week," he said just then. The husky note in his voice sent a delicious shiver down her spine before he deliberately taunted, "Gaby."

Paul Reed, she decided as she marched off to the subway station, was a very irritating man. Since that was the only real certainty to come out of the morning, she was stunned that she'd put up so little fuss about living with him even on such a temporary basis. She was not an impetuous woman. While working on

Wall Street had demanded a certain amount of risk-taking, her decisions were always well-informed, not reckless. So why on earth had she agreed to move in with a man like Paul Reed, a man who made her usually sensible head spin? During the subway ride back to Manhattan, she told herself he'd caught her in a weak moment, with little money and a lease that was about to expire. She even blamed it on the zinnias.

Now, after a blast of cool air and a little distance, she was thinking more clearly. That knot of uncertainty in her stomach was sending a message. She ought to listen to it. She would call and cancel their agreement. No, forget calling. His voice would sizzle across the phone lines and she'd agree to something else ridiculous. It was far more sensible not to show up. It would teach him a valuable lesson about good business. He should have insisted on a lease. He should have asked for references, a deposit. Quite possibly he'd considered the fox coat adequate. If only he knew. It was the last thing of value she owned and she could very well be forced to hock it if things didn't turn around soon.

Pleased with her decision to forget all about the apartment in Brooklyn and about Paul Reed, she pulled the classified ads out of her purse and began to search for another, more suitable apartment, one with a tub where it belonged and no overwhelmingly masculine roommate. But before the subway even crossed into Manhattan, her spirits sank. She could not bear the thought of looking at another dump. The brownstone which, like her, was at a turning point in its life seemed increasingly attractive. And Paul Reed, she decided, she could manage.

"How bad could it be?" she murmured under her breath, hoping for a stronger sense of conviction. It was only for a month after all. Four weeks. She'd handled stock portfolios worth millions. She'd dealt with avaricious, rakish men. She could handle anything for four weeks, even a man like Paul Reed. Starting Monday she'd double her efforts to find a new job. Within a month or two at the outside, she'd be back on her feet and back in Manhattan.

An image of Paul Reed's bold, impudent smile danced across her mind. The subway suddenly seemed much warmer. Doubts flooded back more vividly than ever.

It was the balance in her checkbook that took the decision out of her hands. When it came right down to it, there was no choice at all. It looked as though Friday would be moving day. She'd just buy a very sturdy lock for the bedroom door.

Now why did you go and do a stupid thing like that? Paul asked himself repeatedly after Gabrielle had left. Oh, sure, he needed the money if he was to keep this restoration on schedule and make the monthly payments on the brownstone, but he could have insisted that she wait another month before moving in. He could even have volunteered to move downstairs with his sleeping bag. He'd lived like a vagrant amid the rubble up here for weeks now anyway. Instead he'd managed to manipulate her into sharing the place with him. Was he suffering from some need to torment himself? Hadn't he learned anything about the unbreachable differences between the classes while he'd been growing up on Long Island? He'd been the housekeeper's son on an estate the size of a country club. It had kept him on the fringes of high society all of his life. The women he'd met had been vain, shallow and spoiled. He'd learned the hard way that they were unsuited to anything but the most pampered way of life.

He slammed a nail so hard it shook the door. Gabrielle Clayton belonged in a place like this the way diamonds belonged in the Bowery. She probably wouldn't last half as long as diamonds did in that neighborhood, either. It would give him a certain perverse satisfaction to watch her try to adapt to a lifestyle she quite obviously considered beneath her.

He'd seen the way she looked at him, too, as if he were no better than a lazy, unambitious handyman. Too many people had looked at him just that way. It was about time he taught one of them a lesson about quick judgments and superficial values.

But why Gabrielle Clayton? a voice in his head nagged. He grinned ruefully. That answer was obvious to anyone who took a good, hard look at her. With her honey-blond hair, delicate bone structure and slight Southern accent, she was a sexy bundle of contradictions wrapped in fur. Scarlett O'Hara and the ice Maiden all rolled into one. She had the kind of wide, dangerous eyes that could tempt a man to the edge of hell. There wasn't a healthy, competitive male alive who wouldn't want to explore the possibilities, to try to ignite a flame that would warm that cool exterior, that would put laughter on those sensuous lips.

All he had to do now was make sure he wasn't the one who got burned.

Two

Her parents!

What on earth was she going to tell her parents about this move? Gabrielle thought with a dawning sense of horror as she listened to her mother cheerfully rattling on about the tea party she'd attended the previous afternoon in one of the gracious old houses overlooking Charleston Harbor.

"I do so love that part of town. I don't know why your father won't consider moving. I suppose it's because this old house has been in his family for generations. I'm all for preserving family history, but is it necessary to live in it? Oh, well, if he won't, he won't. Did I mention that Townsend was there?"

When Gabrielle didn't respond, her mother prodded, "Gabrielle, dear, are you there?"

"What?"

"Is something wrong, dear?"

"No, of course not, Mother." She injected a note of cheery bravado into her voice. "Everything's just fine. What were you saying about Mrs. Lane's tea party?"

"I was telling you that Townsend stopped in. He asked how you were," she said pointedly.

"That's nice."

"Don't you want to know how he is, dear?"

"Not particularly."

"Gabrielle!"

She rolled her eyes. "I'm sorry. Of course, I want to know how he is."

"He misses you, dear. I'm sure of it, even though..."

"Even though what, Mother?" she responded on cue.

"Well, I wasn't going to tell you, but since you ask, he's been seeing Patricia Henley."

"That's nice. I'm sure she's much more suited for life with Townsend than I ever was. She actually likes those awful horses of his."

There was an audible gasp on the other end of the line. "Gabrielle, what is the matter with you? It's not like you to be so sarcastic."

"I wasn't being sarcastic. Townsend is happiest on the polo field, as you perfectly well know. Patricia adores horses. She's been riding since she was five."

"We gave you riding lessons," Elizabeth Clayton said stiffly, her voice filled with hurt.

"And I hated them. You didn't fail me, Mother," she said more gently. "You and Father offered me an opportunity to learn all of the social graces. Can I help it if I preferred the *Wall Street Journal*?"

It was a tedious and all-too-familiar conversation. It did, however, serve as an excellent delaying tactic. Any minute now her mother would hang up in a huff.

Coward! The accusation nagged at her. "Mother," she began, interrupting further news of Townsend. "Mother, I really do have to go. I'm busy packing."

"Packing? Where are you going, dear? You haven't mentioned a trip. Are you coming home?" she inquired, her voice suddenly excited. "Oh, it will be so good to see you. Your father and I miss you terribly. We worry about you up there in that awful, dangerous city."

Guilt was now added to cowardice. "Actually, no, I'm not coming home. I'm..." *Blurt it out, Gabrielle!* "I'm moving."

"Oh, are you? It's about time." Whatever disappointment her mother was feeling that Gabrielle was not coming home was now tempered by swift and obvious relief. "I've always thought that apartment of yours was much too small. Whoever heard of living in a single room? I don't care if it is on Park Avenue, that apartment doesn't suit someone of your background. Why, the closet in my bedroom is bigger than that."

That was certainly true enough. It had been specially built to accommodate Elizabeth Clayton's designer wardrobe, which included enough hats to supply every woman who turned out for the annual Fifth Avenue

Easter Parade. It was not that her mother was a frivolous woman. She simply needed the trappings to feel secure in Charleston's more elite social circles, from which she'd once been excluded. Gabrielle had learned long ago to tolerate the excesses, since her father actually enjoyed them. It gave him frequent opportunities to indulge his still-beautiful and adoring wife. He'd learned to his chagrin that similar gifts were wasted on his daughter. She preferred lessons in financial management and subscriptions to business magazines.

"The new apartment is larger," Gabrielle said cautiously, hoping that would be enough information to appease her mother's curiosity. If her mother even suspected the existence of a man like Paul Reed, she'd be on the next flight to New York, clucking over her endangered chick.

"Two bedrooms in fact," Gabrielle added.

"How wonderful! Your father and I will come for a visit soon, now that you have room for us. Tell me all about it. Where is it? Is it a new building, one of those skyscrapers? I'm sure the view must be quite spectacular."

"We'll talk about it later," Gabrielle hedged, already regretting the impulsive disclosure. She couldn't very well explain that the second bedroom was going to be very much occupied or that the building predated her birth and quite possibly her mother's. Mentioning that it was in Brooklyn would definitely arouse more discussion than she could possibly cope with.

"It will take me a while to get settled and do some decorating." *Talk about understatements.* "I have to go now, Mother. Give my love to Dad. I'll call you soon."

"But, dear, you haven't given me the new address or phone number."

"I'll call you with it later. The phone's not even installed yet. Bye, Mother. I love you."

She hung up quickly, before her mother could force her to divulge any more details. Her mother could have been used by the military. She had ways of extracting the most personal disclosures when you least expected it. Once, right in the middle of a conversation about Gabrielle's high school geometry homework, she'd gotten her to confess that there had been boys at Melinda Sue Wainwright's slumber party. She still didn't know how her mother had done it. She'd learned, though, that it was best not to prolong a conversation with her mother when she was trying to protect any intimate secret.

She wondered if she could avoid talking to her at all until after this sojourn in Brooklyn ended.

On Friday morning Gabrielle took a last look around her elegantly furnished studio apartment on Park Avenue. She was going to miss the thick gray carpeting, the glass-topped dining-room table, the outrageously expensive leather convertible sofa, the mahogany wall unit that hid stereo, television, VCR and compact disc player. She was even going to miss the dreadful modern print that hung in the tiny foyer.

She had rented the apartment at the height of her all-too-brief success on Wall Street, at a time when she'd been thumbing her nose at her protective family. After seeing her very first Manhattan apartment, another studio with a less pricey address, they'd begged her to come back to Charleston. They'd reminded her that she could live there in style as a member of high society. She would not have to eat her dinner perched on a sofa, her plate on a coffee table that barely came up to her kneecaps. She definitely would not have to sleep on that very same sofa. There were nights when she couldn't find one single comfortable spot on that two-inch mattress that she was tempted to do as they asked.

However, had she returned they also would have expected her to marry stuffy, rigid Townsend Lane, who was destined for greatness, according to her father. Her refusal to set a wedding date had disappointed them. She doubted if it had had any effect on Townsend at all. He'd barely noticed her when she was there. He'd taken her breaking off of the engagement with his usual cool disinterest and gone off to Palm Beach to play polo with Prince Charles.

If her parents had considered her breaking up with Townsend foolish, they found her business ambitions unladylike in the extreme. Women in the Clayton clan were supposed to inherit wealth—as her father's sweet, but mindless sisters had—or marry it, as her mother had. They weren't supposed to set out to attain it for themselves. She had disgraced them by doing just that, first with a Charleston brokerage house, then by moving to New York where she could avoid their disapproving, bewildered looks.

After the fuss they'd raised about her leaving home, she had sworn to make it on her own. Even at the out- set in New York, she'd refused all their offers of money. She had weathered one stock market crash, only to lose her job a few weeks ago in a subsequent belt-tightening. Unfortunately there were plenty of other stockbrokers and analysts in similar straits, all fighting over the same few openings. Her savings had dipped precariously low. Even so, she knew she couldn't go home again. She would suffocate under all that well-meaning interference. Ten minutes at home and she would revert to being six again, instead of a cool and competent twenty-six.

She pressed the button on the intercom that con- nected her to the lobby and requested a taxi. It was an extravagance she could ill afford, but she refused to tote her belongings all the way to Brooklyn on the subway. Besides, it would take at least five trips just to get them downstairs. She refused to make twice that many trips back and forth to Brooklyn. She convinced herself that in the end, the taxi would be more cost- effective.

In the lobby she said goodbye to the aging door- man, who'd taken to watching out for her. He had the manners of a well-trained butler, all icy propriety, with a glimmer of affection that dared to show itself in lit- tle kindnesses.

"Now you be careful, miss," he said when he'd tucked her into the front seat of the cab after helping the driver to load the trunk and back seat with luggage and boxes. "Stop by now and then."

"Thank you, Robert. I will. You stay inside on rainy days now. You don't want your arthritis acting up. Next time I get over this way, I expect to see pictures of that new grandson of yours."

The washed-out blue of his eyes lit up. "You can be sure I'll have a whole collection of them by then," he said. "Goodbye, miss."

"Goodbye, Robert."

As the cab pulled away, she was surprised to discover a tear rolling down her cheek. She brushed it away and watched until Robert went back inside and the building disappeared from view.

Thankfully the cabdriver, a burly man about her father's age, wasn't the talkative kind. He left her to think about endings and beginnings and all that went on in between. She was feeling gut-wrenchingly nostalgic all of a sudden. The driver, Mort Feinstein according to the ID tag located on the glove compartment door, glanced over occasionally. Gabrielle caught the growing concern in his expression and avoided meeting his gaze directly.

As they drove into the neighborhood of the new apartment, the driver's concern turned to alarm. He pulled to the curb in front of number six-blank-two and stared around disapprovingly.

"It's not safe," he decreed.

"No place in this city is safe. I'll use locks."

"And stay inside? You shouldn't walk down the streets. Take a look around."

"Please, no lectures. Just help me unload my things."

"You're a nice girl. I can tell you're from a fine family. What would they think, they should see this?"

"They won't see it."

"You know what I mean. What you want, you want your father should have a heart attack, he finds out you're living in a neighborhood you can't go out in even in daytime."

"It's not that bad," she said, getting out and slamming the door. She opened the back door, began removing things from the back seat and piled them up on the sidewalk. Still shaking his head, the taxi driver began getting the suitcases out of the trunk.

"You stay here," he said. "I'll take them inside. What floor?"

"Four."

He rolled his eyes.

"I'll help," she volunteered.

"If you help, who'll watch? Stay."

Just then Paul emerged from the building. His jeans were just as faded and just as snug as the ones he'd had on when they'd met, but he had buttoned his shirt either in honor of her arrival or in concession to the near-freezing temperature. He smiled at her, a slow, breathtaking smile that made her wish for a minute that he was her lover and that they were embarking on a mad, passionate affair.

Without saying a word, he took the full load of luggage from the taxi driver. Mort looked him over carefully, then nodded. He turned to Gabrielle. "Maybe it'll be okay."

"What was all that about?" Paul asked when the taxi finally had pulled away and they'd hauled everything up to the fourth floor landing.

"He doesn't think I should be moving into this neighborhood."

Paul opened his mouth. She spoke first. "I don't care to have this discussion with you, too."

"Fine." He nudged the door open with his foot and stood aside for her to enter. She found...chaos. At least she hoped that's what it was. Surely it couldn't be his idea of furnishings.

A sofa that sagged dangerously in the middle had been shoved against one wall. Two chairs in a similar state of disrepair were situated haphazardly in the middle of the room. None of the pieces matched. An orange crate had been placed in the midst of this unlikely arrangement. A mayonnaise jar filled with marigolds had been plunked in the middle of it. As a gesture of welcome, it was a nice touch. As decor, it was frightening. She was terrified to look in the other rooms. Squaring her shoulders resolutely, she walked down the hall.

Each bedroom had a twin-size bed with a mattress that dipped in a way that set off desperate warning signals in her back. There was a scarred four-drawer dresser in each room. Each had a jar of marigolds on top. At least he was consistent, she thought with a sigh.

She dropped her suitcases in the room with the least offensive bedspread—pink chenille with a minimum of tufts missing. She would have to use the tiny dressers in both rooms and both closets for her clothes. She might not have her mother's acquisitive nature, but she did own more than two dresses. Maybe Paul could at least keep his clothes downstairs while he worked on the apartment.

When everything had been dragged inside, she turned to Paul. "If you'll just give me my keys now, I'll start settling in and you can go on doing whatever you were doing before I arrived."

He dropped the keys in her hand, picked up more of her bags and hauled them down the hall.

"Thanks, really, but I can manage the rest of this," she protested.

"No problem. Until we get these things out of the way, we'll just be stumbling over them."

"Don't you have work to do downstairs?"

"Not today. I took the day off so I could welcome you properly."

Gabrielle was just picking up a box of dishes when the seductive undertone to his words registered. She dropped them. The crash of Limoges didn't even faze her. "Welcome me?"

"Yeah," he called over his shoulder. "I'm glad you like the pink room. I figured you would. I'd already put my stuff in the other room."

"Why would you want to welcome me?" she said, regarding him suspiciously. "We have an arrangement. That's all. You come and go as you please. I come and go as I please."

He grinned at her. "Does that mean you don't want lunch?"

Before she could say a strenuous no, her stomach rumbled. "Okay. Fine. Lunch would be good. We can iron out the details of the arrangement and make a schedule for the kitchen."

"Whatever you say."

In the kitchen there were more marigolds on the counter. A bottle of wine had been opened, an omelet pan was on the stove and she could smell French bread warming in the oven. Her mouth watered. She tried not to notice that the wallpaper was still peeling.

"Is there anything I can do?"

"Nope. It's all under control, unless you'd like to pour the wine."

"Sure. Where are the glasses?"

He nodded toward the cabinet to his left. "Up there."

She found four jelly glasses with cartoons on them and a stack of plastic cups. Well, why not? The wine would taste just as good from a glass with little yellow Flintstone characters on it as it would from her Waterford. She selected the two that matched and poured the wine, then handed Paul his glass.

"Shall we have a toast?" he asked, glancing over at her.

"To what?"

"Roommates." His gaze lingered on her until she felt heat rise in her cheeks. Her heart thumped unsteadily. "And friends."

Before she could protest, he tapped his glass to hers and sipped the wine. "It may not be French, but it's not bad."

Gabrielle wondered at the defensive tone, then taunted back, "I prefer California wines myself." She grabbed two mismatched plates from the cupboard and turned around to set the table...only there wasn't one.

"Where...?"

"We'll have to eat in the living room, unless you'd like to go outside. I think it's warm enough today for the garden, if we stay bundled up. The sun's just getting around there."

The garden. Perfect. Just the thought of it brought a smile to her lips. "We'll go outside."

She loaded up everything she could carry and went downstairs. Paul followed minutes later with the steaming food. When they'd finished the cheese and mushroom omelets, the entire loaf of French bread and a bowl of grapes, he slid lower in the chair, stretched his powerful legs out in front of him and stared at her as he sipped his wine.

"You should spend more time outdoors," he said finally. "You're too pale."

"Haven't you heard? The sun is bad for your skin."

"Use sunscreen and moderation. It'll put a little color in those cheeks. You could add a couple of pounds, too. You've probably been starving yourself."

"I have not been starving myself, thank you very much, and my figure is no concern of yours."

"I'm the one who has to look at it."

"You don't have to. In fact, I'd prefer it if you didn't. Remember our deal."

"Our deal was that I'd stay in my own room at night. There were no restrictions on what I'd do during the day."

"Which brings us to something very important. We need to set a schedule."

"I don't do schedules." The response was deceptively soft and pleasant. She had a feeling it hid a mulish personality.

"If this is going to work, we have to have a schedule," she said firmly. "You can't just come barging into the kitchen when I'm..." She could not bring herself to complete the thought.

"Fixing breakfast?" he offered with a grin.

She scowled. "No, dammit. When I'm taking a bath." She struggled for a businesslike demeanor. "Now, it seems reasonable that I have the use of the kitchen in the morning, since I have to go out on job interviews. You probably like to bathe at the end of the day anyway. So that should work out nicely."

He was shaking his head.

"What's wrong?"

"I take two baths a day. Morning and night."

"Why?"

"Habit."

"Break it."

"Two baths."

It was hard to argue with cleanliness. "Okay, fine. Take your damn bath in the morning. Just make sure you leave me some hot water and be out of the kitchen by seven-thirty."

"I eat breakfast at seven-thirty."

"Where? In the tub?"

"At the counter, standing up. Toast, cereal, eggs and coffee."

"That's not healthy. You need to sit down and digest your food properly. You can eat your breakfast in the living room."

"But I always . . ."

"If you want your morning bath, you will eat your breakfast in the living room."

"That's blackmail," he retorted.

"That's compromise," she growled.

He grinned. "Okay."

She regarded him suspiciously. "You're agreeing?"

"I just said I'd do it, didn't I? Who's going to do the dishes?"

"We're each going to do our own."

"That means I'll have to come back into the kitchen, while you're . . ."

Oh, dear heaven! "Never mind," she said, gritting her teeth. "Leave the dishes. I'll do them."

"Then what do you want me to do to even things out?"

"Nothing."

"I'll fix lunches for both of us," he went on as if she hadn't spoken.

"I won't be home for lunch."

"You can take it with you."

"I prefer to eat in restaurants."

He tilted his head knowingly. "Can you afford to do that right now?"

"No," she admitted reluctantly.

"Fine. Which do you prefer, peanut butter or tuna fish?"

"Yogurt."

"On a sandwich?"

Patience, Gabrielle. Have patience! "No. In its own little container. I'll pick some up when I go to the store."

"Don't you think we should go to the store together? For the next few weeks, I mean. If we combine groceries, we'll both save. Right?"

She supposed it did sound practical. "Okay. We'll make up a list when we go back upstairs."

"Who needs a list? We'll just go and get whatever appeals to us."

"That's inefficient and expensive. We'll end up with things we don't really need and we'll forget some of the basics."

He stared at her solemnly. "You need to loosen up. Do you put everything in your life on little lists?"

"Not everything," she said stiffly. He was, however, remarkably close to the truth. She didn't have much patience with wasted motion.

"That's a good way to miss out on what's important."

"It works for me."

He shrugged. "If you say so. Now there's one thing we haven't talked about."

"Which is?"

"Guests. What do we do if we want to have someone over?"

"You mean like a date?" The mere thought of it raised all sorts of awful possibilities she hadn't considered. She supposed a man like Paul would date a lot. She also imagined he wouldn't leave those dates at their own front door with a chaste peck on the cheek. The thought stirred a little agony of uncertainty deep inside her. She met his amused gaze.

"Yes, a date," he said softly.

"Can't you wait until you move into your own apartment?" she grumbled.

"I'm willing to compromise here, but let's not go nuts about it. Don't you date?"

"Of course, I do, but it won't kill me to meet my dates in a restaurant for the next few weeks."

"And after?"

"After what?"

"After dinner?"

"We'll each go to our respective homes."

"Sounds sensible." The way he said it, it sounded like a death sentence. He cast a meaningful look at her. "I'm not that sensible."

"Fine. If you are unable to curb your male hormones for a few weeks, just let me know and I will arrange to be out for the evening."

"For the night," he corrected.

Of course, it would be for the night. She seethed. "I will not be kept out of my own bed for an entire night."

"I don't mind, if you don't," he said easily. "I guess that settles everything."

"Yes. I guess it does." Why had all this talk of dates left her feeling empty and alone all of a sudden? She enjoyed living alone. She was perfectly capable of entertaining herself. She had her collection of CDs and tapes, her videos of her favorite movie classics, and a stack of unread books. Let Paul Reed go out tonight. Every night, for that matter. She'd be just fine. It would be good to have the apartment to herself... until he came home with these dates of his.

She stood up suddenly and began snatching the dishes off the table.

"Something wrong?" Paul inquired innocently.

"Of course not. What could possibly be wrong?"

"You seem upset."

She slammed the dishes right back on the table. "I am not upset. Nothing is wrong. I am going upstairs to unpack, if you don't mind."

She stalked away from the table, then turned back. "Thank you for the lunch," she said politely.

He was grinning. In fact he looked rather pleased with himself. "You're welcome," he said softly.

To her unreasoning fury, she heard the quiet lilt of his laughter as she stormed up the stairs. This was going to be the longest damn four weeks of her entire life.

Three

———

Paul couldn't sleep, not with those provocative sounds emanating from Gabrielle's room next door. Apparently she'd taken him at his word and had invited a date over on her very first night. So much for all of those self-righteous protests of hers.

In an attempt to give her some of the space she so obviously wanted, he'd spent the rest of the day away from the apartment. He'd hoped, on his return, that she would be settled in and that his own rampaging hormones would have quieted down. At first he'd been relieved that she was already in her room with the door closed. He wouldn't have to put his libido to the test. Then, as he'd stripped off his shirt, he'd heard the soft music, the low, intimate murmur of voices. Something had knotted painfully inside him.

Retreating to the kitchen for a beer, he'd told himself it didn't matter. Gabrielle Clayton was a roommate, a source of income. That was it. He had absolutely no personal interest in what she did with her evenings. He told himself it was good that he saw her for exactly the kind of woman she was from day one. He told himself to go to bed and forget all about her.

Fat chance!

He stared at the ceiling, his imagination running rampant. The messages it sent to his body were not restful. He flipped on his own radio, found a station playing quiet, soothing music...all about romance. Why didn't somebody just play lullabies at night? He turned the dial and found a classical station. The music was soft and just as romantic, but at least there were no words. He closed his eyes, thought about the lulling rhythm of waves against the shore and felt the tension in his body begin to fade at last.

Then, just about the time he finally began to drift off, he heard the start of a rhythmic thumping from next door. He groaned and buried his head under a pillow. It didn't shut out the music or the other far more tantalizing sound.

What in the hell was she doing in there? Never mind. He knew what she was doing. He could picture it all too vividly, her long legs sleek and bare, her golden hair spilling across the bed, her body slender and urgent.

He groaned and debated getting another beer. At this rate she'd drive him to alcoholism within a week. Telling himself it was his own fault was no comfort at all. Telling himself there was absolutely nothing he could do about it without seeming like a meddling, jealous jerk didn't quiet his tightly strung nerves, either. Telling himself he could not possibly survive an entire night of this torture motivated him to get out of bed, yank on a pair of jogging shorts and risk humiliation by pounding on Gabrielle's door. He acted quickly, before he could think about the consequences.

"Keep it down in there," he yelled, then stomped back toward his own room.

With surprising speed for someone engaged in such heated activity, she flung her door open and stepped into the corridor. He hadn't counted on that. It stopped him right in his tracks, unable to do any more than stare at her as his pulse throbbed. Her face was flushed, her hair mussed. Her chest was heaving. His entire body tightened in immediate response. Knocking on that door had been the second stupidest damn mistake of his entire life, topped only by inviting her to live here in the first place. If listening had been torment, witnessing her sensual arousal was pure agony.

"I'm sorry," she said breathlessly. "I had no idea you could hear me. I didn't even realize you'd come home."

"I'm not surprised," he said.

Apparently the sarcasm escaped her. She continued to regard him with wide, innocent eyes. "I couldn't sleep," she explained, "so I had my radio on for a while, but it didn't help. Then I got to thinking about how I've been missing so many aerobics classes and, since I couldn't sleep anyway, I thought I'd just run through the exercises. I'm sorry if the tape woke you."

As the significance of her explanation sank in, Paul felt his entire body go slack with relief. "Aerobics?" he said, hoping that the grin spreading across his face wasn't nearly as silly as it felt. "That's what you were doing in there?"

"Of course. What did you think?" Her eyes widened, then sparked with amusement. She bit back a chuckle. "You didn't?"

He stared back indignantly, still fighting his own grin.

"You did, didn't you? You thought I had someone in there." Then she began laughing, the first genuine, honest emotion he'd ever seen from her. It was a glorious sound. She peeked at him and started chuckling all over again.

"Okay," he grumbled. "So I got it wrong. Just go back to bed."

She swallowed back another laugh with effort. "I told you. I can't sleep."

"Count sheep."

"It doesn't work."

"Try reciting the names of all the states and their capitals."

"I want to sleep, not test my memory. If I miss one, I'll be up the rest of the night trying to remember it."

"I'm sure the aerobics won't help. Your blood's probably pumping so fast right now, it'll be hours before you settle down. Try some warm milk."

"We don't have any. We never did get to the store today." She smiled at him enticingly. "Since you're awake, too, we could play cards."

"Bridge, I suppose?"

"Poker."

He hesitated. The idea of playing poker with a half-dressed woman in the middle of the night held a certain appeal. Too much appeal. If he had a grain of sense, he'd go out for the blasted milk instead. "Do you have any cards?"

"Of course," she said, going immediately to a box that had been carefully labeled with every item in it.

"That much organization is probably illegal. When you move, you're supposed to lose things."

"Who says?"

"It's a law of nature or something." He led the way into the living room and gestured toward the orange crate. "You deal. I'm getting a beer. Want one?"

"Beer sounds good."

That surprised him, but he made no comment. Nor did he say much when she displayed an extraordinary knack for knowing when to hold her cards and when to fold 'em. When she folded for the fifth or sixth time in a row, Paul grew frustrated.

"Why not play the hand out?"

"It's always better if you know when to cut your losses."

"We are not playing for the rent money. Hell, we're not even playing for matchsticks."

"If you get out of the habit of playing like you mean to win, it'll get you in trouble later."

"And who taught you that bit of wisdom?"

"My father. He swears it's how he made his first million."

"His first million?" Paul repeated with a dry inflection. "Exactly how many does he have now?"

Gabrielle shrugged sleepily and took another sip of beer. "Ten. Twenty. I don't know. He doesn't think it's important for women to know those things."

"If your father has all that money, why are you living here?" Paul asked, thoroughly bemused. He'd known Gabrielle was classy, that until very recently she'd had some money, but he'd had no idea just how much.

"Because *I'm* almost broke," she explained patiently.

"But your father—"

Her chin set stubbornly, though the effect was lost in a yawn. "That's his money," she said, continuing to shuffle the cards.

It finally dawned on Paul that there was some sort of pride at stake here. "Your father doesn't know you're running out of money, does he? How long before the next trust fund check comes through?"

"What trust fund check?" She put the deck of cards down in front of him. "Cut."

Still perplexed, Paul did as she asked. So there was no trust fund, he thought as she dealt. Yet she didn't seem to be estranged from her family. The fondness she felt for her father had been unmistakable in her voice. She had quoted him not with irony, but with respect. Figuring out the complexity of the relationship was something he decided to leave for another time.

They played a few more hands before he got up and went for another beer. When he came back into the living room, she was sitting on the floor, legs tucked under her, her head resting on the orange crate.

"Gaby?"

She gazed up at him with sleepy eyes and a suggestion of a smile on her lips. All at once playing poker and her family's elusive financial dealings were the last things on his mind. He tried to tell himself the swift sexual reaction was perfectly understandable. He hadn't fully recovered from that earlier misinterpretation of the noises in her room. He reminded himself sternly that he had no personal interest in Gabrielle Clayton beyond her ability to pay the rent.

Then he made the mistake of picking her up and carrying her back to her room. She snuggled. The woman curled up in his arms, buried her face against his neck and smelled like some exotic flower. He wanted to drop her onto her bed and escape just as quickly as he possibly could. Instead he put her down gently, then stood watching her, wondering at the vague tightening in the pit of his stomach. This woman wasn't cool and distant. This woman wasn't a snob. She was warm and vulnerable and desirable. And he needed to get very far away from her very fast.

The room next door wasn't nearly far enough. Gaby might have been sleeping peacefully in her own bed, but she made her presence felt in his dreams. He blinked awake to incredible loneliness and throbbing memories.

Well, hell, he thought, staring at the ceiling for the second time that night. He might have been tempting fate by inviting her to share this apartment. He might even have hoped that the chemistry between them would prove irresistible. But he hadn't planned on feeling this tender protectiveness at all. In fact, quite the opposite. He'd been absolutely certain that daily doses of her disdain would fuel his natural aversion to women who thought they were too good for the average man. Instead she hadn't been in the apartment twenty-four hours and already his carefully erected wall of preconceptions was cracked at the foundation. It made for a very long night.

Gabrielle did not want to get out of bed. It was Saturday morning. From the brightness of the sun slanting through the window, she judged it to be a beautiful day. But Paul was very likely to be in the next room and she wasn't sure she was at all prepared to go another round with him.

Every one of their encounters had disturbed her in some indefinable way that went well beyond irritation. Their latest, in fact, was a dim but decidedly pleasant memory. She recalled the strength of his arms around her, the gentleness of his touch, the oddly haunted look in his eyes when he'd thought she'd been with another man. She wasn't sure which was likely to be more difficult to face, the impossible man she'd first met or the tender one who'd helped her through the night. Such uncertainty had a tendency to make her cranky.

Finally she dared a trip to the bathroom. Fortunately Paul didn't seem to be anywhere in the apartment. In the bathroom, however, she was reminded emphatically of his presence. She found his damp towel laying on the floor, his razor beside a sink dotted with specks of dark hair and his T-shirt on the door handle. The intimacy it suggested sent a little shiver dancing along her spine. That made her mad, though admittedly out of all proportion to the seriousness of his transgression. It also helped her to put that single incident during the night into its proper perspective once and for all. She was rooming with an inconsiderate slob, not some knight in shining armor.

She cleaned the sink, washed up, dressed, picked up his belongings and tore open the door with every intention of dumping the items in the middle of his bed. She hadn't counted on practically tripping over him. He was lying in the middle of the kitchen floor, his very bare upper body partially hidden in a cabinet. Unfortunately quite enough was exposed to tease her imagination. She dropped his things on his stomach and heard a muttered exclamation, a thump and then a curse.

He emerged rubbing his head and peered at her balefully. "What's the story?"

"There is one bathroom in this apartment."

"How observant of you to notice," he retorted, responding to her admittedly nasty mood. "What's the problem?"

"I will not clean up after you."

"You don't have to."

"Well, we sure as hell don't have a maid to do it."

"Right again."

"I will not live in a pigsty."

He carefully removed the assortment of items on his stomach, holding them up for inspection. "I'd hardly call one towel, a razor and my underwear the makings of a pigsty."

"It's a start."

"Come on, Gaby, loosen up. I'm used to living alone. We'll have to work out the details as we go along. I'll buy a medicine chest for the razor. I'll install a towel rack later. As for my underwear, if that disturbs you . . ." he began with a leer.

"It doesn't disturb me!" She was practically shouting.

He grinned. "Then why are you shouting?" Paul couldn't resist chuckling at her furious expression. It was good to see yet another break in that cool, controlled facade of hers. In fact, if it weren't so dangerous to his own equilibrium, he might make that his immediate goal, seeing to it that Gabrielle Clayton exchanged what had apparently been a rather uptight existence for something a little more carefree. Even now her frown wavered uncertainly. He had a feeling that now that she'd told him off, she wasn't quite sure what to do next. Politeness dictated an apology, but her mood obviously did not.

"Come on," he said, putting aside his wrench and his common sense. He got to his feet and held out his hand.

She regarded him warily. "Where?"

"We're going to brunch."

He caught the quick flash of interest in her eyes before she shook her head. "We can't. There's too much to do around here."

"It can wait."

"I cannot live in total chaos."

"You can work twice as hard on a full stomach."

"I don't have money to throw away on brunch when we can cook right here."

"I do. Besides, there's no food in the refrigerator except for some cheese that's turning green."

She swallowed hard at that. "Okay. But we're roommates. We go dutch or not at all."

"Not this time. We're celebrating."

"What?"

"Our first fight."

"It's not our first," she said with the beginnings of a smile. "We've been arguing since we met."

"Then it's time we called a truce." He grinned at her. "Over brunch."

She caved in sometime between his deliberately provocative description of fresh-squeezed orange juice and the promise of waffles and warm maple syrup.

"One hour," she agreed finally. "No more."

"Relax, Gaby. If you eat too fast, you'll get indigestion. Isn't that what you told me yesterday?"

"An hour," she insisted, glaring again.

"Do you want to time it down to the second?" he inquired, offering her a view of his watch. She scowled back, yanked on her jacket and descended the stairs like a queen on her way to court.

"Where are we going?" she asked, turning back at the corner to wait for him.

"I thought you knew," he retorted. "You're leading the way."

She slowed her steps and grumbled, "Don't you ever hurry?"

"Not if I can help it. Stress is bad for you. Don't you ever slow down?"

"You can't afford to in my business."

So, he thought, she really hadn't been taking money from her father. "What is your business?" he asked, envisioning an elegant boutique on Madison Avenue struggling against exorbitant rents and fickle tastes.

"I'm a stockbroker."

Stunned, he simply stared at her.

Oblivious to his astonishment, she bit her lip. "Actually, I was a stockbroker. Now I seem to be having trouble convincing people of that."

Paul tried to reconcile his first impressions with reality. "Were you any good?"

"I was damn good."

"So why'd they fire you?"

"Who says they did?"

"You don't seem like the type of lady who'd walk away from a sure thing with no prospects in sight." And yet, in many ways, that was exactly what she'd done when she'd left the family nest.

"You think you have me all figured out, don't you?"

"Not really," he said honestly, gesturing to a crowded deli at the same time. "Is this okay?"

"Fine."

He gave his name to the hostess, then turned back to Gabrielle. "Well? What happened?"

"Okay, I was fired." The sparks in her eyes dared him to make fun of her for that. "Not because I wasn't good, though. It's just that there were dozens who were better and who'd been there longer."

"If the business is all that tight, what makes you think it'll be any better at another brokerage house? You could work your tail off and end up out of a job again, right? All through no fault of your own."

She shrugged, her expression resigned. "It's a risky business."

Curious about her unemotional tone and the flat, empty look in her eyes, he said, "Why do you do it?"

"I trained for it. It's what I do. You hammer and paint. I sell stocks and bonds."

"Why?"

She ignored the question as they were finally led to a table. As soon as she was seated, she buried her face behind the menu. It didn't take a genius to figure out she was avoiding the question. As soon as their orders had been taken, Paul persisted. "Why, Gaby? What is it about the stock market that turns you on? Is it the money, the power, the risks? What?"

Her gaze narrowed defensively. "You sound as though you disapprove of making money."

"Hey, what's to disapprove of? Money's great and it's none of my business what you do with your life. I just see a woman who's existing on nervous energy, who can't sleep at night, who's living in an apartment she considers to be not much better than a slum—"

"I never said that."

"It's in your eyes, sweetheart. They're the windows to the soul, remember. They'll give you away every time."

She immediately looked chagrined. Rudeness apparently was inconceivable to someone of her unfailingly polite Southern upbringing. Every time she crossed the boundaries of what she considered polite conversation, she looked guilty. And apologized.

"I'm sorry," she said, right on cue.

"Hell, you don't have to be sorry on my account. I like where I am. I like who I am. What about you? What does it take to make you happy, Gabrielle Clayton?"

"Success," she said instantly, but that trace of uncertainty was back in her eyes.

"How do you measure success? By the number of shares of stock you've sold? By the size of the portfolios you handle? By the takeovers you've manipulated? When you played Monopoly, were you only happy when you'd bought up all the real estate?"

She looked uncomfortable with the question. "I wanted to win, if that's what you're asking. Don't you?"

"Sure, but I only compete with myself. I don't have to conquer the world."

"We're all entitled to different goals."

"Don't patronize me, Gaby."

She flushed guiltily again. "That's not what I was doing."

"Wasn't it? I'm sure you think it's just terrific that I'm content when the paint goes on smoothly. Isn't it nice that Paul can be happy with so little?" When she started to deny it, he shook his head. "Those eyes again, sweetheart. They say it all."

"And what about your eyes?" she snapped back. "You've jumped to a few conclusions about me, too. Rich. Spoiled. What else, Paul? What labels did you stick on me at first sight?"

He slumped back in the booth and grinned ruefully. "Touché. Maybe we ought to start all over again without any preconceptions."

"Why?" she asked softly. "In a few weeks I'll be out of your life. What we think of each other won't matter at all."

"Are you so sure of that?" he responded just as quietly, not sure why he was so quick to defend the possibility of a future for them.

He saw the heat rise in her cheeks, caught yet another glimmer of uncertainty in her eyes. "Never mind. We've gotten entirely too heavy for an outing that was meant to relax you. Let's play hooky for the rest of the day and just have some fun."

"But the apartment, all those boxes, you promised to get the medicine chest and the towel rack . . ."

He heard the token resistance in her voice, saw the wavering resolve in her eyes and wondered how long it had been since she had allowed herself the simple pleasure of an afternoon off.

"Tomorrow will be soon enough, Gaby."

A spark of irritation flared in her eyes and something else, a surprising wistfulness. It confirmed his suspicion about the lack of stolen moments she'd captured for her own joy. He played to that tiny hint of vulnerability.

"Please," he coaxed, "Gabrielle."

Four

―――――

Despite its brightness, the sun hadn't taken the crystal sharp bite out of the fall air. Gabrielle shivered as they strolled toward the subway entrance at Paul's favored leisurely pace. Seeking warmth, she poked her icy hands into the pockets of her denim jacket. She should have worn the fox coat, but it would have looked out of place with her jeans and sweater. It would also have underscored the vast differences between herself and Paul. His idea of style seemed to consist of clean jeans, an unrumpled shirt and a sheepskin jacket that was several years removed from the sheep.

"Come on," he said, apparently noticing the effect the brisk air was having on her. "It's freezing out here. I'll race you."

Gabrielle's prompt protest was lost as he took off with the loping, natural stride of an athlete. She sputtered indignantly, but was too much of a competitor to ignore the challenge. By the end of the block, the cold air hurt her lungs and her side ached, but she was filled with the strangest sense of exhilaration. Her whole body felt alive with anticipation.

Paul grinned at her and she found herself smiling back, suddenly more lighthearted than she'd felt in years. It was a beautiful day, her housing problem was temporarily resolved and until Monday there was not a thing in the world she could do about finding a new job. Paul was a handsome, sexy companion with a sense of humor. Why not enjoy this day, this moment?

"That run put some color in your cheeks," he said approvingly.

She shook her head with feigned impatience. "What is this fixation you have about my coloring? Did you have aspirations for being a doctor?"

"No medical hopes at all," he said, taking a slow step toward her. Gabrielle's breath caught in her throat as he reached over, caught a strand of her hair and tucked it behind her ear. The unexpected gesture startled her with its tenderness. His rough knuckles grazed her cheek and sent warmth flooding through her.

"It's not your coloring," he said, his intent gaze lingering. "It's your health I'm worried about. You don't take care of yourself properly."

"And you still want me to ride the subway?" she retorted. She was teasing, but she was unable to hide the slight catch in her voice.

"Now, with me, you're perfectly safe," he promised in a voice that could have seduced a saint.

Their gazes collided. Her pulse beat erratically and she wondered just how true his statement about her safety actually was. The instinct to run was powerful, the temptation to stay even stronger.

They spent the rest of the day exploring Paul's New York. It wasn't the same part of the city Gabrielle had grown used to seeing. Instead of the elegance of Lincoln Center, they wandered through the colorful seediness of Chinatown. The narrow, crowded streets smelled of garlic and ginger and incense. Shop windows were jammed with displays of gaudy trinkets side by side with graceful Oriental antiques. In one, buried beneath worthless porcelain vases, Gabrielle spotted a small silk rug, its colors muted by age, its fringe tattered in spots. Despite its worn appearance, it appealed to her sense of proportion and color.

"Oh, Paul, it's perfect," she exclaimed.

"For what? A dust rag? It's decrepit."

She glared at him. "No more than our apartment building."

Only after the words were out of her mouth did she realize that she'd actually sounded proudly possessive about the still shabby Brooklyn apartment they'd shared for less than twenty-four hours. From the quizzical expression on Paul's face, she knew he'd noted the slip of her tongue.

"Really, don't you think it would be perfect for one of the bedrooms?" she said hurriedly.

He looked skeptical, but said agreeably, "If you want it, get it."

Once inside the store, however, the price daunted her. It would put a significant dent in her savings, though from what she knew of Oriental carpets, it was not outlandishly high. Making a quick calculation in her head, she made a decision. She told the smiling proprietor she would pay him half what he was asking.

"No, no. Not possible," he said, his expression suitably horrified. "Price firm. No discount. It is very valuable. Fine silk. Good workmanship."

Gabrielle examined the rug closely, then dropped the edge in exaggerated disgust. "It needs repairs. I will have to pay at least half what you're asking just to clean and restore it."

He could hardly deny the truth of that. Reluctantly he knocked the price down by a fourth. Gabrielle glanced at Paul and saw the amused quirk of his lips.

"Another fifty dollars and we have a deal," she said with finality.

The man looked as though she were trying to rob him. "No, no, lady. That is too much."

Gabrielle sighed heavily. "Okay," she said, and started for the door. She took one last, longing look at the carpet. Then she noticed Paul's dismayed expression, just in time to keep him from intervening. She grabbed his hand and dragged him purposefully toward the exit before he could offer to pay exactly what the man was asking in a misguided attempt to please her.

"But—" he protested.

"Don't you dare make an offer," she whispered. He stared disbelievingly, but kept quiet.

They were in the street when the proprietor caught up with them. "Okay, lady, we make a deal."

She gave Paul a smug smile and followed the man back inside. When she'd written her check, he rolled and wrapped the carpet with loving care before handing it over to Paul to carry.

She held in her delight until they reached the corner, then turned and grabbed Paul's arm in excitement. "Can you imagine? He actually sold that carpet to me for a fraction of what it was worth."

"But you said . . ."

She waved aside his obvious confusion. "I was bargaining."

Paul shook his head in astonishment. "You really must have been good on Wall Street. I'd never have guessed from your expression that you were cheating that poor old man."

"I wasn't cheating him," she explained patiently. "He probably got it for even less than that. He knew what he had to get to make a profit and I guarantee you, I didn't get him below that."

"But you will still have to pay for cleaning and repairing it."

"Don't be silly. I'll hang it over a tree limb and beat it. I can stitch up the fringe myself."

Paul stared at her, openmouthed.

"What's wrong now?"

"You. In the first place, I would never have expected you to be satisfied with anything less than brand-new and top of the line."

"You have a lot to learn about the value of antiques," she countered.

He ignored the barb. "Okay, but I definitely would never have imagined you bargaining over the price of something."

"How do you think rich people stay that way?"

He rolled his eyes. "Fine. I'm sure you learned those tactics at your daddy's knee along with poker, but the idea of your sitting down with needle and thread completely boggles my mind."

She grinned at him then and adopted her most Southern accent, the one that called to mind hamhocks, black-eyed peas and grits. She laced it with the sweetness of honeysuckle. "Why, Paul, honey, don't you know we gentlewomen always learn sewing and piano along with the social graces."

He winced. "Sorry. I did it again. Is there anything about you that fits the image or can I anticipate constant surprises?"

"You won't be surprised, if you remember I'm Gabrielle Clayton, not Scarlett O'Hara or Faye Dunaway in *Network*."

A fleeting frown gave away his guilt. She wondered which of the personae he found the more disconcerting—the Southern belle, born to the manor, or the sharp-witted career woman. Or perhaps it was the seemingly contradictory blend of the two. Whichever it was, he tried to cover his confusion by quickly pointing her in the direction of a bakery in Little Italy. "As a reward for your success, you get coffee and dessert."

The thought of food so soon after their huge brunch held no appeal. Normally her breakfasts consisted of coffee and half a grapefruit, her lunches of yogurt and her dinners of fish and a salad. She frequently forgot all about one or more of those. Today she'd already eaten more calories than the three meals combined. "Not for me," she said. "I'm still stuffed."

He pulled her inside the warm, fragrant bakery anyway and led her straight to the display case. "Maybe you can resist one of these sinfully rich, chocolate cannoli, but I can't. I have to give in to temptation once a day or I feel I've failed to live up to my image as a hormone-driven rogue."

The pointed rejoinder, reminding her that she'd made a few snap judgments of her own, shut her up.

Paul picked out the creamy pastry, then compounded the temptation by ordering capuccino. "Sure you don't want some?"

"No. Absolutely not. Just a cup of black coffee."

"It's bad for your nerves. How about decaf?"

She looked at the waitress. "Black coffee, loaded with caffeine."

The waitress glanced deferentially at Paul, earning a scowl from Gabrielle. "Whatever the lady wants," he confirmed. "But bring two forks, just in case."

Seated, with the cannoli in front of her, Gabrielle's resistance diminished considerably.

"Try it," Paul urged, cutting into the pastry. Chocolate and cream puffed out the ends. She swallowed hard. He held the bite in front of her. Her mouth watered. "Come on. We'll walk it off."

Challenged by determined blue eyes, she took the bite at last, slowly licking the cream from her lips. It was heavenly. "Mmm."

"Another one," he tempted.

"No, really." But with the taste lingering on her tongue and Paul's eyes still intent on hers, her usually indomitable willpower faded. Before she realized it, she'd eaten the entire cannoli. She glanced at the empty plate and blinked guiltily. "Oh, dear. I'm sorry."

He laughed. "For what? They have more." He signaled the waitress for another order. "You sure you won't want your own this time?"

"Very funny. I wouldn't have eaten the last one, if you hadn't tempted me."

"Are you that susceptible to temptation?" he inquired with a devilish gleam in his eyes.

"Only before four o'clock in the afternoon on the fourth Saturday in months that begin with O."

He glanced at his watch and gave an exaggerated sigh of disappointment. "I'll mark my calendar for next year." Grinning, he sat back, sipped his capuccino and studied her. "What would you like to do now?"

She hesitated, uncertain of his interests or his budget and aware of a surprisingly strong desire to accommodate both. Usually she scoured the weekend events listings in the papers on Friday, then planned exactly how she would spend her all-too-rare free time. It was about as spontaneous as the ticking of a clock.

"It's up to you," she said, experiencing a daring sense of excitement that was all out of proportion with the innocence of the situation.

"How do you feel about art?" he asked, taking her by surprise again.

"Modern or classical?" she replied enthusiastically. She'd taken one art history course in college to fulfill what she'd considered to be a totally frivolous requirement. She'd enjoyed the class far more than she'd expected to and once in New York had indulged the fascination with regular visits to the museums and galleries. She was on the invitation list for the openings of all major showings.

"Take your pick," Paul offered. "We can go to the Metropolitan or the Museum of Modern Art or we can go to a couple of places I know."

She was instantly intrigued by the prospect of discovering what type of art interested him. "The places you know," she said at once.

He smiled his approval, then led the way to Soho, where each gallery's art was more wildly imaginative than the one before.

"Well," he said thoughtfully as they stood in front of a sculpture made of clock and auto parts. It was called *Ride to the Future*. Gabrielle recalled the reviews. One critic had described it as "banal and lacking in excitement."

"What do you think?" he inquired with what she assumed had to be feigned solemnity.

"You can't be serious." She stared at his face for some indication he was merely teasing her. He met her gaze evenly. "My God, you really are serious."

"That's right. Don't just dismiss it. Tell me what you really think of it."

"I think..." She walked around the display, viewing it from all sides and perspectives, trying very hard not to be influenced by what she'd read or her own taste for far more traditional works. This was definitely not Michelangelo's *David*.

"I think it's an interesting concept," she concluded finally, trying to squirm off the hook.

"Well executed?"

"I suppose." She couldn't keep the doubt from her voice.

"But not to your taste?" he said at once.

She sighed and admitted reluctantly, "Definitely not."

She waited for some expression of disdain for her lack of daring. Instead he nodded in satisfaction. "Good. I thought it looked like a piece of junk, too."

Gabrielle was startled into laughter. "I thought you loved it."

Amusement lit his eyes. "I know. I wanted to see how politely you could decimate it."

"For a minute there I was terrified you might be the artist."

"Trying not to insult the artist, huh? You succeeded admirably. My favorite word when I get invited to these shows is *interesting*. It's amazing how many inflections you can give that word to convey everything from approval to dismissal.''

"*Fascinating* is good, too. Or how about, *I've never seen anything quite like it before.* Delivered solemnly, it's very effective."

Their amused gazes caught, sparks danced and the laughter slowly died between them. "Amazing how much we've already found we have in common," Paul said with a disturbing mixture of satisfaction and defiance in his tone.

"Amazing," she echoed softly, when what she really felt was fear, not amazement. Already she was struck by the sense that this man could turn her life in a totally unexpected and dangerously fascinating direction. He wasn't easily intimidated. Nor was he fitting neatly into the niche she'd carved for him. And when he looked at her, every bit of common sense ingrained in her since birth fled.

She reminded herself staunchly that she was in control, that the parameters of their relationship had been clearly drawn. They were short-term roommates, nothing more. And Paul, she sensed even after their short acquaintance, was an honorable man. Satisfied that their bargain was unbreachable, she relaxed her guard again.

It was nearly midnight when they got home, after eating spicy Mexican food in Greenwich Village and drinking far too many margaritas.

Gabrielle felt just as exhilarated as she had in the morning and slightly tipsy. She couldn't recall the last time she'd had so much uninhibited, unstructured, spur-of-the-moment fun. Nor was she feeling particularly guilty about it. How extraordinary!

"Thank you," she said as they stood in their darkened living room.

Impulsively she stood on tiptoe to brush an appreciative kiss across Paul's lips. In the hushed silence she suddenly heard the pounding of her heart, the sharp intake of his breath. Then she looked into Paul's eyes and saw the unmistakable darkening of desire, felt her own blood race. As their breath mingled, she knew if she touched the warmth of his lips, even just this once she'd get burned. There were limits, even in the midst of magic. The idea that they could remain simply roommates, that their emotions would remain impassive, fled with the blink of an eye. The sense of destinies irrevocably entwining overcame her again.

Paul's well-muscled body, tight with tension, was suddenly too tempting, too overpowering. Shaken, she backed away a step, the friendly kiss abandoned as a very bad idea.

"You're running again, Gaby," he said with heart-stopping accuracy.

"Gabrielle," she said with a touch of her old defiance.

His lips curved into a faint smile. He ran a finger along her jaw. "Gabrielle," he said in a whisper so soft it caressed as gently as a spring breeze. Her resistance turned to liquid fire as he moved toward her. Her whole body trembled in anticipation.

"You promised," she said with a broken sigh as he bent closer. Still, despite the nervous plea, her lips remained parted for the kiss, waiting, longing. The mere sensation of anticipation was one she'd denied herself for too long. It sang through her veins.

At her protest, though, a shadow passed over Paul's features and he straightened slowly, reluctance etched on his face. "So I did."

He settled for running his fingers through her tangled, wind-tossed hair, the light touch grazing her cheeks. Her body ached from the tension of wanting more and knowing that satisfaction of that need would be wrong for both of them.

The expression in his eyes was regretful as he whispered, "Sweet dreams, Gabrielle." Then he turned and went straight to his room without a backward glance.

Paul's body was hard and charged with the urgency of his desire to claim the woman who slept in the next room. In just a few hours curiosity had slipped into fascination and was quickly turning into something much stronger. It wasn't supposed to have been this way, but he should have known it would be. He'd always wanted things that weren't his to take.

It had been hellish for a small boy to discover that the toys his friends took for granted would never be his. His mother had been a housekeeper, his father a gardener. Honest, kind, hardworking people, they had loved him all the more because he had come along late in their lives.

Because of his parents' jobs, he had grown up on a huge estate on Long Island. His playmates had been the children of the manor, children just like Gabrielle

Clayton. No matter how hard he'd tried to be one of them, though, they were always just beyond his reach. He wore their cast-off clothes and he dreamed their dreams. But for him those dreams were unattainable. At age five, the differences had been insignificant. By twenty they'd torn at his gut. That was when he'd realized with irrevocable and heartbreaking finality that Christine Bently Hanford would never really think of him as anything more than the son of the hired help.

It had taken him ten years away from there to get over the anger, to find his own niche, to become comfortable with who he was and what he wanted out of life. Envy and bitterness had faded, replaced by contentment. Or so he had thought until Gabrielle had appeared on his doorstep. Was he still trying to capture the unattainable? To prove he was good enough? If that's what he was doing, he was being unfair to himself and to her.

Then again, maybe she was just a lady who was going through the same sort of identity crisis that had torn him apart ten years ago. He'd learned to live with reality, rather than fantasy, to find satisfaction in what was, rather than what he wished life could be. Maybe he could teach Gabrielle the same lesson.

And then what? Could they live happily ever after? Not likely. That happened only in storybooks, where Cinderella was swept away by the handsome prince. No one ever wrote about what happened when the prince woke up to reality and found out Cinderella was no princess.

This story—his and Gabrielle's—would end now, before anyone got hurt. He smiled in the darkness, his lips touched with irony and the sensible finality of the decision.

Famous last words.

Five

────

With a disconcerting sense of déjà vu, Paul awoke to the thumping of furniture. He smiled. Then a sudden crash from the room next door was followed by a surprisingly extensive barrage of colorful words. Paul would have sworn Gabrielle Clayton had never heard that particular vocabulary at home, except possibly during one of those infamous poker games. He leaped out of bed and ran for the door, stopping just in the nick of time to tug on a pair of gym shorts.

When he got to Gabrielle's bedroom, he pushed on the door, but it wouldn't budge. He panicked, pounding on the door. "Gaby, are you all right? What happened in there?"

There was no response.

"Gaby?"

"Go away," she muttered finally, sounding thoroughly disgruntled.

"Gaby, sweetheart, open the door," he pleaded more gently. He suspected the persuasive tone was about as wasted on Gabrielle as it would have been on a three-year-old who'd locked herself in the bathroom. "I just want to make sure you're okay."

"I am perfectly fine," she growled. "Just go back to sleep."

Paul's panic began to recede in the face of her spirited responses. Now he was simply curious. "How can I possibly sleep when it sounds like war has erupted in the room next door? Do you need any help?"

"No. I can handle this."

"Handle what?"

"I'm just rearranging things a little."

"With dynamite?"

"Very funny."

"That furniture's too heavy for you to manage alone. Wouldn't you like a little help? Open the door."

He heard her mumble something and suspected it was another of those words. "What did you say?"

"I said I can't open the damn door."

"Why not? Is it locked? I have a spare key. I'll slide it under the door."

"It's not locked."

"Is it stuck?"

"No, dammit."

Amused by the mixture of irritation and fierce pride he detected in her voice, he inquired lazily, "Well, if it's not locked and it's not stuck, what's the problem?"

"The bed's in front of it."

He chuckled.

"Don't you dare laugh."

"I'm not laughing," he swore, fighting the urge to do exactly that. "Just move the bed."

"Oh, for heaven's sake, don't you think I would if I could?" she snapped.

Paul bit back another laugh. "Gabrielle, exactly what is wrong in there?"

"I was trying to put down my new rug," she began after a lengthy pause. Her voice trailed off forlornly. That odd note in her voice concerned him as nothing else had. Gabrielle Clayton forlorn? Defeated by an inanimate object?

"And," he encouraged.

He could practically hear her taking a deep breath before she said in a rush, "I moved the bed and then the chest fell over and now I'm sort of trapped in here."

Any desire to laugh died at once. "Under the damn chest?" he demanded, his voice rising in panic again.

"Sort of," she said softly. "Oh, hell, I was so sure I could do this on my own."

"Just wait there," he said soothingly before he realized the utter absurdity of the order. Of course she would stay right where she was. What else would a woman with most of her bones crushed do?

Without giving it a second thought, he raced through the apartment, down the steps and around the building to the fire escape. He was halfway up when the icy metal against his bare feet registered. Suddenly he realized exactly how ridiculous he must look climbing a fire escape in gym shorts on a morning when the temperature could not possibly be much above freezing. It wasn't something he had time to worry about, though. Gabrielle might even be going into shock. She'd sounded pitiful and frail there toward the end, when she'd finally admitted she was trapped. That tone of voice was definitely unusual for her.

He reached the bedroom window and tried to lift it, peering through the glass for some sign of Gabrielle under the hodgepodge of furniture. He saw bare toes and a slender calf. He followed the curve of her leg upward, trying not to linger over it, and encountered—the chest of drawers, on its side. Only the fact that a corner had snagged the edge of the bed on the way down had kept it from landing on top of her with its full weight. His breath caught in his throat and his heart seemed to stop right then. The silence inside that room seemed particularly ominous. Impatient with the stuck window, he shattered the glass, oblivious to the cuts on his hand.

At the sound of glass breaking, Gaby shouted at him. "Don't you dare come in here and bleed all over my new carpet."

His heart began pumping again.

"Did you hear me?" she called out. "No bleeding."

He grinned at the feisty warning. She must be improving. "I heard, but I don't give a damn about your carpet," he said, feeling suddenly more cheerful. "Just stay still until I can get to you. I have to be careful where I step because of all the glass."

"Aren't you wearing shoes?"

"Sorry. I didn't take time to stop and dress formally. Think of this as a come-as-you-are party."

"What are you wearing?" she asked curiously.

"Shorts," he said curtly.

"That's all?" She definitely sounded better. In fact, she sounded downright perky.

"Be thankful I'm wearing those. At least it's probably enough to keep the neighbors from calling the cops about the crazed nudist on our fire escape. Now before I lift this chest up, does anything hurt?"

"Mostly my pride."

"Sorry. I'm afraid you can't afford any just now."

He lifted the chest up slowly, making a frantic grab for the drawers as they slid forward. He just barely kept them from tumbling out on top of her.

Once the piece of furniture was righted and out of the way, he saw that she'd been trapped not so much by the weight of the chest as by that damnable carpet. It was wrapped halfway around her, pinning her arms to her sides, raising all sorts of interesting possibilities. He knelt down beside her, trying very hard not to stare at the rounded swell of her breast peeking from the top of a very sexy nightgown. That view fueled those possibilities more effectively than matches and gasoline.

"You're not dressed," he said, his choked voice laced with surprise and sudden uncertainty. His mind was screaming *off-limits* so loudly his head hurt. It wasn't the only part of his body responding to the intriguing combination of sensuality and indignation before him.

"I hadn't planned on having company," she retorted dryly. "I might add that my body is covered more adequately than yours."

Paul had a horrible feeling that was all too true. Fighting embarrassment and desire and a whole new meaning of panic, he freed her from the carpet with swift, trembling fingers, then shoved the bed aside. He noticed that she seemed to be holding her breath, her eyes wide as they met his. A man could get lost in those eyes.

"Get dressed," he ordered brusquely as he left the room.

"Aren't you going to help me clean up the mess?" The laughing request followed him down the hall, daring him to stay. He wondered how often Gabrielle was tempted to play with fire.

"Later." Perhaps after he'd taken vows of celibacy.

He went back to his room, grabbed his clothes and practically ran through the apartment to the bathroom. En route he regarded the tub balefully and promised himself that he would install a shower in every one of the apartments the minute he had the money... even if he could only supply it with cold water. That was all he was likely to use for the next few weeks anyway.

Gabrielle was filled with confusion as she watched Paul storm off. She hadn't realized at first that he really was furious. Otherwise she would never have teased him after he'd come to her rescue. Why on earth had he gotten so upset? She certainly hadn't meant to get trapped in her room. And, given time, she probably could have extricated herself. She hadn't damaged the battered old furniture, for heaven's sake. And how much could it cost to replace a pane of glass?

Of course, the swift reversal of his mood from concern to testiness might have had something to do with the highly charged atmosphere between them. Even she had to admit that it was incredibly disconcerting to keep tripping over their physical attraction. She had not been immune to the flying sparks just now. Her own pulse was just beginning to settle back into its normal rhythm.

Well, there was nothing to be done about that except to ignore it. They simply couldn't allow another quiet, intimate moment like last night's to occur. Of course, if this morning was any indication, perhaps they shouldn't be together in the same room—even in broad daylight. If Paul truly felt that uncomfortable in her presence, then maybe he should consider moving downstairs.

That decided, she put on her jeans and a soft rose-colored sweater before venturing into the kitchen to make coffee. She heard Paul swearing in the bathroom. When he threw open the door and caught sight of her at the stove, he just glared and stomped on past. Moments later she heard the front door slam.

"I guess he doesn't want breakfast," she muttered, searching through the refrigerator for something edible. She poked at a loaf of bread that was definitely past its prime. There was a package of luncheon meat that had dried out and curled on the edges. In fact, the only thing that appeared to have been purchased more recently than the Stone Age was a bottle of catsup. She sighed and settled for the coffee.

Paul returned before she'd taken the first sip of her coffee. He was carrying the Sunday paper and a bag, which he dropped on the orange crate. "Bagels," he announced abruptly. "If you want one."

"Thank you."

"Any coffee left?"

"On the stove."

"Thank you. Do you want any more while I'm getting it?"

"No, thank you."

The politeness was beginning to grate on her nerves. She grabbed the front section of the paper and hid behind it. Bad as they were, the headlines were less depressing than the awkward wariness between the two of them.

Still, when Paul returned, she said politely, "Did you want to see the front section of the paper?"

"No. I'll read the sports section first."

"Fine." When she'd finished, she reached for the rest of the paper. Her hand collided with Paul's. Startled, they both looked up as if they'd made contact with a live electrical wire. "Sorry," they said simultaneously.

Gabrielle wondered if all relationships went through cold wars like this, wars that erupted for no apparent reason and sizzled with tension. She opened her mouth to force a confrontation, but Paul's forbidding expression silenced her. Now wasn't the time. Instead she got to her feet, took her dishes into the kitchen and washed them. As she was heading back to her room, Paul called to her. She walked to the doorway.

"Yes."

"Sorry. I shouldn't have snapped at you earlier."

"No problem," she said. When he turned back to the paper, obviously satisfied that the matter was concluded, she went on down the hall, torn between puzzlement and irritation. The apology had acknowledged the situation, but it certainly hadn't resolved it. Her own failure to pursue the matter was an indication of how thoroughly out of her element she felt.

As the morning went on, Paul's mood didn't improve, though eventually he did come down the hall to help her move the furniture back into place and sweep up the shards of glass. As they worked they exchanged a minimum of conversation, all of it exceedingly polite. When they'd finished, he pulled on his jacket and headed for the door.

"Where are you going?" she asked, then remembered it was none of her business. "I just meant in case someone calls."

"I'm going to get new glass for the window."

"Then let me give you some money."

"I broke it. I'll pay for it."

"You broke it on my account."

"Forget it, Gaby. Just sit down and relax. Read the paper or something."

"What about groceries?"

"What abut them?"

"Shouldn't we go to the store today? Or would you rather I go alone?"

He sighed heavily. "Get your coat. We might as well go now."

She opened her mouth to remind him that they hadn't made a list, then clamped it shut again. If they forgot something, they'd get it later. In his present mood Paul was unlikely to want to discuss the relative merits of green beans versus broccoli before he'd even reached the produce section.

At the store Paul grabbed a shopping cart and steered it deftly through the narrow, crowded aisles to the dairy case on the far side of the store. "We'll work our way back."

"But we should do this last," she protested.

"Why?"

"It'll spoil."

"Not unless it takes you all afternoon to shop."

She glared at him. "Okay. Fine. What do you want?" she said as she grabbed a package of butter and a triangle of Brie. He picked up a block of cheddar cheese and a tub of margarine.

"Eggs?" she asked.

"Yes."

She reached for brown eggs. He shook his head adamantly. "Eggs are supposed to be white."

"You don't eat the shells," she reminded him, "What's the difference?"

"If there's no difference, then you might as well get the white ones."

She picked up a half dozen of each, then stalked off to the cereal section. She had a box of oat bran in her hands when Paul arrived with the cart.

"What's that?" he inquired suspiciously.

"Oat bran. It's good for your cholesterol."

"I eat cornflakes."

"Can't you just try this?"

"I have always eaten cornflakes."

Gabrielle threw up her hands in resignation. "Fine. If this is some nostalgic thing for you, we'll get cornflakes."

Suddenly his lips twitched. She felt the first tiny break in the tension.

"I suppose you have a thing about bread, too." She recalled that the loaf in the refrigerator had once been white. He nodded. She sighed. "We'll get white and whole wheat."

As they approached the meat section she said, "What about dinners? Do they have decent fish here?"

"Beats me."

"What do you eat?" she began, then held up a hand. "Wait. Let me guess hot dogs and steak."

He grinned. "What else?"

"You're going to die before you're forty."

"As long as I don't do it while we're sharing the apartment, it shouldn't bother you."

"Couldn't we make a deal for the next few weeks? I'll do the cooking and you'll try whatever I prepare."

He glanced down at the groceries they'd already collected. "Okay," he said finally. "But none of those funny looking green things."

Gabrielle's mind went blank. "Funny looking green things?"

"You know, they look sort of like a cactus."

"Artichokes?"

"Yeah. That's it."

She bit back a laugh. "Okay. No artichokes. Anything else?"

"No fish eggs."

"I wouldn't dream of wasting caviar on you."

"And we go out for pizza one night a week, so I won't starve to death."

Laughing, she held out her hand. "It's a deal."

After an instant's hesitation, he took her hand. "Deal," he said softly, his gaze locked with hers. It was not a look meant to be shared over raw hamburger. It spoke of candlelight and white damask napkins. Or maybe satin sheets.

She knew without any explanation that the truce had to do with far more than artichokes and caviar. Paul, a man whose life had probably been quite simple only a few days ago, was struggling to find the right balance for their complex and confusing relationship. That handshake was his renewed commitment to try.

But despite the pact in the grocery store, the day continued to have moments of high tension, moments when a glance threatened to turn into far more, moments when a casual remark took on added meaning. Paul's edginess communicated itself to her until they were practically tiptoeing around the apartment to avoid offending each other.

Finally Gabrielle retreated to her room and sat down with the classified ads. Moments later she heard Paul leave the apartment. Her heart sank to the pit of her stomach, but she forced herself to concentrate on the ads. She already had two interviews lined up for the following morning. Both were for jobs she'd heard about by word of mouth. Still she looked, circling one or two that she'd at least call about.

"And what if these don't pan out?" she said aloud. "How long are you going to wait before taking Paul's advice and looking for something different?"

One more day, she promised herself finally. If Monday's meetings and calls failed to result in at least a strong possibility of a job offer, she would turn elsewhere. To remind herself of the commitment, she folded the classified section and placed it prominently where she couldn't miss it, propped against the mayonnaise jar of flowers that had barely survived the morning's calamities with petals intact.

She decided it was time to replace them. A visit to the garden might also soothe her frazzled nerves and keep her out of Paul's way. If he was going to growl around like an angry bear, it was definitely wise to stay out of his path.

Unfortunately he found her.

"We need to talk," he began at once, sitting down in the chair opposite her. He picked up one of the flowers she'd cut and began stripping it of its petals.

"Okay," she agreed cautiously, moving the remaining flowers out of reach. "What about?"

"Our..." He hesitated, refusing to meet her eyes.
"Our arrangement."

"Does that include an explanation about why you've
been in such a foul humor ever since this morning?"

"You noticed?" he said with a touch of wry humor.

"That doesn't necessarily qualify me for a Ph.D. in
psychology. So, what's the story?"

"We have a problem."

"Already? I've only been here two days."

"That's long enough."

Gabrielle drew in a sharp breath. The response was
hardly unexpected, but disappointment began some-
where deep inside and settled around her heart. "Are
you suggesting that I leave?"

He hesitated far too long before answering. "No,"
he said finally. "I asked you to move in. I certainly
don't want to turn right around and throw you out."
He sounded very stoic. She wanted to throttle him. In
fact she might have, if he hadn't looked quite so mis-
erable and confused. "It's just that we have to reach
some sort of understanding."

"About what?"

"This relationship."

"That's easy. We don't have one." The remark was
glib, but there was considerably less conviction in her
voice than she would have liked.

"Exactly."

She didn't pretend to misunderstand the all-too-
adamant response. "I think I see what you're getting
at. Every now and then our bodies take over and pretend they haven't gotten the message that we're off-

limits to each other, that we're coming from different places, heading in different directions. Is that it?''

"Yes. I mean you're an attractive woman. A man would have to be dead not to respond to you, even though he knows it's an impossible situation.''

"And you are far from dead," she concluded.

"Exactly."

"Would it help if I wore baggy clothes?''

He grinned at that. "I don't think so. I have a feeling you could wear a gunny sack and I'd see right through it. So to speak," he amended.

"Any other suggestions?''

He stared at her helplessly, then shook his head.

She considered their situation analytically. Normally it was something she was very good at. "Maybe we're going about this all wrong. Maybe we should just get this right out in the open. You're attracted to me. I'm attracted to you. We both know we shouldn't do anything about it, so that makes it forbidden and, therefore, all the more interesting.''

He held up a hand to interrupt her. "There's only one problem with that particular logic. Taken to its natural conclusion, we should just go right ahead and explore the possibilities and see where these feelings take us.''

Gabrielle swallowed hard. The idea had far more merit than she cared to admit. Every time she glanced at Paul's strong hands, she recalled the magic in his most casual caress. She glanced at them now and her skin burned. "I see what you mean," she said shakily.

"You think we'd be in even more trouble than we're in now."

"I know it," he said with such conviction that she smiled.

"Okay, I'm open to suggestions." She leaned forward, eyes wide, and propped her chin in her hand.

Paul's eyes widened and he leaned away from her hurriedly. "Don't do that."

"What?"

"Look so damnably inviting. You could tempt a man to ruin with that look."

She did laugh at that. "If something's going to happen between us, it will be with our mutual consent, right? Since you want to keep this strictly platonic and so do I, we should have no problem. We're not a couple of lusty kids with no sense. It should be even easier beginning tomorrow. You'll be back at work. I'll be job-hunting. We probably won't even see each other."

He seized on her logical, unemotional comments with transparent relief. "Absolutely. That's right." He got to his feet looking far more relaxed than he had when he'd joined her a half hour earlier. She was surprised he didn't hold out his hand to be shaken. He was even whistling when he went back inside.

So, she thought when he had gone, it was all out in the open. Discussed and resolved exactly the way it should be between two rational, mature adults who knew a mistake when it stared them in the face.

Now all they had to do was live with it. And that was complicated by the realization that with every hour that

passed, she was having more and more difficulty recalling why she and Paul were so terribly wrong for
each other. It sure as hell didn't have anything to do
with artichokes. She didn't like them, either.

Six

In the morning their unemotional, carefully conceived plan went wildly awry.

Still half-asleep and suffering from a splitting morning headache that she blamed totally on Paul's seductive invasion of her dreams, Gabrielle wandered barefooted into the chilly kitchen. She began running water for her bath, only dimly aware that there seemed to be plenty of hot water. Yawning, she slipped off her robe and climbed into the tub, sinking slowly down into the luxurious warmth. She slid lower, sighed and rested her head against the back of the tub. Some of the tension began to ease in her shoulders and neck.

The she heard a door open. The bathroom door! Not five feet away. And only one person could possibly be opening that door at this hour of the morning, unless a particularly fastidious burglar had stopped in to shave.

"Paul, don't you dare come into this room!" Admittedly overly hysterical and definitely wide-awake, her screech echoed off the walls and made her head throb even more.

The door slammed shut, the noise like a shotgun blast reverberating through her head. She prayed he was on the far side of it.

"Dammit all, Gaby, we had a schedule."

He had retreated. But even through the door, she could hear that his indignation was tempered by a slight breathlessness. Apparently her warning shout hadn't been quite in time to prevent a very thorough look at her unclad body. The temperature in the kitchen seemed to warm by several degrees, setting her cheeks aflame.

"I forgot it," she said with unaccustomed meekness as embarrassment washed over her.

"It was your schedule. You wanted me out of the kitchen by seven-thirty. It is now seven-twelve."

"Okay. So I didn't look at the clock. Are you going to kill me over eighteen measly little minutes?"

"I wouldn't if I were anywhere other than trapped in this bathroom. Get out of the tub. You'll have to finish your bath later, after I've had mine."

She did not want to get out of this water, now that she was in it. She knew instinctively that there was not enough hot water in the entire building to give her a second bath this temperature. "Give me ten minutes. That's all."

"Out," he repeated with stubborn insistence. "You're on my time."

"Five minutes," she bargained, reaching hurriedly for the soap.

"Forget it. I have to get to work. I'm already running late. I might as well forget about my own bath. I'll be doing good just to make it across town. I am coming out now."

It occurred to her that for a man she'd pegged as irresponsible, he was suddenly awfully conscious of time management. Under the circumstances, the turnaround seemed extraordinarily suspicious.

"Don't you…" She began the warning with haughty indignation. It failed her as she heard the latch click. She stared at the opening door with a growing sense of incredulity and dismay. He was actually coming out. Wearing a towel and a frown. Her heart thumped unsteadily. His arms and shoulders were every bit as muscled as she'd imagined. His stomach…well, never mind. His stomach was much too low and definitely too bare for a lady to be studying.

Then she considered her own predicament. She glanced down. There were no bubbles in this water. No frothy covering. Not even a bar of soap floating on the surface. Come to think of it, there wasn't even a towel nearby. She hadn't been nearly alert enough to remember to bring one. Towels belonged in bathrooms. Then, again, so did tubs. Logic aside, the fact of the matter was that there probably wasn't a decent covering within twenty or thirty feet. In his current belligerent mood, she certainly couldn't count on Paul to supply one . . . except perhaps for the one he was wearing and that would create far more problems than it solved.

"Paul Reed, if you're going to insist on walking through here, then you can at least close your eyes," she said imperiously, lifting her gaze—very hurriedly—to clash defiantly with his. It was a tactic she'd seen her mother use with extraordinary success with everyone from her father to the gardener. They, however, had not reacted with the same amusement that played about Paul's lips.

"If I close my eyes, I'm liable to trip and join you in that water," he pointed out, clearly unimpressed by the command in her tone. In fact, he looked as though he was beginning to enjoy her discomfort.

She switched to a heartfelt plea. "Then look at the counter. That'll guide you right out of here. Please."

It was only after he'd done just that with her watching him warily, that she realized she was essentially trapped in the kitchen—in the damned tub—until he left the apartment. Of course, she could retreat to her room soaking wet, leaving a trail of water for Paul to complain about and wearing a silk robe that, when wet, would reveal almost as much as it concealed. Or she could break down and request a towel.

She was still debating the relative merits of the alternatives when she heard a sharp intake of breath behind her. She held her own breath for the impatient outburst that was sure to follow.

"Dammit, Gaby, aren't you out of here yet?"

She sank lower in the now murky, icy water. She wanted very badly to respond to the exasperated tone. She wanted almost more than anything to tell him exactly where he could go with his badgering and his self-righteous indignation. She wanted to lambast his insensitivity to her predicament. She wanted to remind him of how any gentleman would have handled the situation.

The fact remained that she needed a towel and there wasn't a gentleman in sight.

"If you'll bring me a towel, I will be happy to get out of your way," she said, substituting stiff formality for angry charges.

To her surprise he did exactly as she asked without a murmur. When he returned, however, he lingered just a shade too long in the doorway. The ragged sound of his breathing warned her of his presence nearby. He was either dramatically out of shape or he'd paused to take in the view. She'd seen his well-toned muscles and bet readily on the latter. He was gawking again. Despite the rapidly cooling water, her skin burned under his slow, thorough surveillance. She recalled the smoldering deep blue of his eyes in the moonlit living room on Saturday night, the quickening then of his breath and her pulse.

Finally she heard his footsteps, soft and coming heart-stoppingly close. Unless his nobility was far stronger than she had any reason to credit him with, he could see quite clearly the tightening of her nipples just below the surface of the water, the bare plane of her belly, the shadowy triangle of hair below. Swallowing hard, she held out her hand for the towel.

"I'll hold it for you," he said thickly.

They both knew it was not a gentlemanly gesture. Far from it. It was temptation. It was daring all sanity. But short of staying stubbornly right where she was so Paul could witness the deepening rose of a blush in her cheeks and God knows where else, there seemed to be little alternative.

Furious, yet undeniably intrigued by the sensations rocketing through her, she shot a quick peek up. The indiscreet glance caught the visible rise and fall of his chest, saw the lines of tension at the corners of his mouth, the blatant hunger in his eyes as he caught her gaze and held it for an eternity.

Just when Gabrielle thought he'd stolen her breath forever with something as simple as a look, he closed his eyes and murmured something that sounded like a cross between a curse and a sigh of regret. He dropped the towel and left, slamming the front door behind him. The sound echoed through her soul.

Surrounded by deafening silence, Gabrielle trembled violently at the nearness of her escape. *Their* escape. She dressed hurriedly and left the apartment with a sense of urgency, trying to leave behind the undeniable thrill of pleasure she had felt for one all-too-brief, maddening moment under his hot, longing gaze. With pesky, troubling persistence, it followed her, creating distraction in its wake.

She remembered her all-important briefcase midway to Manhattan. She snagged her last pair of expen-

sive hose on a torn subway seat she would ordinarily
have been alert enough to avoid. She filled out the first
two-page job application with visibly shaky handwrit-
ing that bore little resemblance to her usual firm script.
For a few panicky seconds she couldn't recall her new
address. During her first interview, she found herself
staring blankly at her prospective employer, unable to
recall his name or his question, but remembering Paul's
face all too vividly.

The interview ended shortly afterward with a non-
committal and unpromising handshake. For the first
time in her life Gabrielle found herself ordering a drink
with lunch. She downed the martini in two quick gulps
and was tempted to order another. Only rigid self-
discipline and the prospect of that two o'clock interview kept her from it. She never touched her salad. Her
thoughts in turmoil, she ripped the crisp French roll
into a mound of crumbs, then stared at the resulting
mess in astonishment.

In the ladies' room, she examined herself in the mir-
ror and caught the confusion in her eyes. No man had
ever taken her so much by surprise. No man had ever
breached her defenses so skillfully, though many had
tried. Worse, Paul wasn't even trying. He was as
shaken as she was by the attraction that warred with an
incompatibility so basic only a fool would ignore it. If
ever their common sense failed simultaneously, however, she had no doubt the resulting explosion of desire would be thrilling beyond imagination. Sadly, their
broken hearts would be destined to lie in the ultimate
rubble of that explosion.

If she were wise, she would move out now. She would take an offer of temporary shelter with one of her friends and make Paul Reed nothing more than a distant memory. Without a doubt, she knew she should go while there were no wounds to heal. And yet....

The hammer slipped, missing the nail and leaving a semicircular gash in the expensive mahogany paneling. Cursing, Paul glared at the offensive hammer. It wasn't his. His was at home, left behind with all of his other tools in his frantic race from the apartment that morning. Rather than returning for them and risking yet another disconcerting encounter with Gabrielle, he'd been borrowing what he needed from the men he'd hired to work with him on this renovation job in an increasingly swank section of Brooklyn Heights.

Still muttering under his breath, he yanked out the few properly placed nails that held the damaged strip of wood, then tossed it aside. He was about to replace it when he heard a nervous cough.

"Uh, boss?"

Only one of his workers respectfully called him "boss." He turned to stare into the concerned eyes of the skinny, blond eighteen-year-old he'd been training as a carpenter's assistant. His own expression softened. Underneath the often cocky demeanor and bitter cynicism, Mike was a good kid. He'd just needed somebody to believe in him, not unlike Paul himself had at that age.

"What's up, Mike?"

"Don't you think maybe you ought to take a break?" he said cautiously.

The comment sounded suspiciously like advice. From a snot-nosed kid no less. Paul's hackles rose.

"Why?" he said. The retort was unnaturally soft. It should have been taken as a warning.

Unused to such subtleties, Mike persisted. "It is time for lunch."

"Then take it," Paul said in a dismissive tone that would have sent a lesser man scurrying. Mike's pimpled chin tilted defiantly. He even risked taking a step closer. A tiny spark of approval flared inside Paul as he waited for the counterpunch.

"You coming?" Mike said hopefully.

"Not now."

Mike drew in a deep breath, but his gaze never wavered. "Maybe you should."

Exasperated, Paul scowled.

"I mean," Mike persevered. "You've already ruined five strips of this stuff this morning." He poked a scuffed workboot at the stack of discarded boards. "At this rate, the job's going to cost you money."

Paul found himself staring at the pockmarked wood as if he had no idea how it had gotten there. He sighed heavily, then grinned. "You may have a point," he admitted finally. "You grab the lunches and I'll run down the block and pick up some soda."

Mike held out one black pail, identical to Paul's own. "I've already got my lunch. I couldn't find yours."

Of course not, Paul thought with wry acceptance. It was still at home in the damned kitchen. Not far from his tools. Even closer to the spot where he had very nearly lost his head and seduced Gabrielle Clayton at seven thirty-two this morning.

Tomorrow he would put the tools and his lunch by the front door the minute he got up. Tomorrow he would be out of the apartment by seven-fifteen and not one second later. Maybe even seven o'clock. Tomorrow, if he was lucky, he would avoid temptation altogether.

Tonight was another story.

Gabrielle's day improved only to the extent that she actually did get home without taking the wrong subway, leaving her purse behind or getting mugged. Beyond that, it could be counted as one of the worst days of her life. The two interviews she'd had—and the others that hadn't panned out—convinced her that she would never work as a broker again. Despite her promise to herself that she would take this as a clear sign to move on to a new challenge, her spirits were at an all-time low.

It didn't help to open the door and see that horrible hodgepodge of furniture Paul had collected. Without removing her coat, she flipped through the yellow pages, whirled around and went back out.

Two hours later, her mood vastly improved, she was back again, stumbling awkwardly up the front steps with her purchases, dumping them in the foyer and collapsing on the bottom step. Listening to the sound of music and hammering, rather than being nervous as she'd expected to be, she was simply grateful that Paul was home to help. She shouted at the top of her lungs to be heard over the noise.

The hammering paused, though some rock tune she didn't recognize blared on. She didn't hear the opening of the apartment door over the din, but she looked up in time to see Paul peer over the fourth floor banister.

"Thank goodness," she said with heartfelt relief.

"What?" He held his hand to his ear to indicate he couldn't hear her.

"I need your help," she shouted.

"What?"

She shrugged and pointed at the collection of items in the foyer, then gestured for him to come down. He approached her slowly with the wariness of a man who expected anything but a friendly reception. He stayed a careful three steps from the bottom, as if he expected to need a head start back up.

"What's all this?" he asked cautiously, staring at the two badly scarred tables and the large bag from a neighborhood hardware store.

"It's for the apartment," she said excitedly, determined to put the morning's awkwardness behind them. "Aren't they absolutely perfect."

"For what?"

"End tables, of course. And I saw this really wonderful sofa. It was an incredible bargain, but I couldn't figure out how to get it home and I decided you might want to take a look at it, too, before we get it."

"Why are you doing this?" He looked thoroughly baffled.

"What?"

"Furnishing an apartment you have no intention of staying in more than a few months."

"Because I'm not sure I can stand looking at what's in there now, even for a few months."

He regarded the tables skeptically. "If you don't mind my saying so, these don't appear to upgrade the quality of the decor by much. How many layers of paint do you suppose are on here?"

"Six," she said readily. At his surprised glance, she grinned. "I counted when I was chipping my way down to the natural wood. I think it may be cherry. Come on. Help me get them upstairs."

"How did you get them this far?" he asked, stacking them on top of each other.

"They didn't walk by themselves, I can tell you that."

He regarded her incredulously, from the fox coat to the tips of her two-inch Italian heels. "And you carried that bag, too? How far did you lug this stuff?"

"Not far. I found the tables in this perfectly marvelous secondhand store about fifteen blocks from here. I picked up the rest at that hardware store a couple of blocks over."

Paul was staring at her as if she'd just declared an ability to lift a moving van by the tips of her fingers. "Are you nuts? Why didn't you call for help?"

"For heaven's sake, it wasn't that far. I had to stop a lot, though," she admitted.

"You and your idiotic streak of independence," he muttered in disgust. "It was far enough to strain your back."

"My back is fine."

"It won't be in the morning."

"That will be my problem, won't it?"

"Not if it means you'll want to soak it in a hot tub," he retorted, staring at her meaningfully. "Call next time, okay?"

"Okay," she said very softly. The gruff concern combined with the all too fiery memories to make her miss a step. She stumbled and only her sharp reflexes kept her from tumbling backward down the stairs. The near-accident snapped her back to reality. She concentrated very hard on reaching the apartment without further embarrassment, then on placing the tables in precisely the right spot. When Paul had them exactly where she wanted them, she nodded in satisfaction, finally taking off her coat and tossing it across the sofa.

"I knew they would work."

"They do, don't they?" Paul said, sounding pleased. "What about the paint?"

Oblivious to her designer suit, Gabrielle knelt down and began pulling cans of paint stripper, pads of steel wool, protective gloves and a container of tung oil from the bag. "The man at the hardware store assured me this was everything we'd need."

"We?"

She gave him her most winsome smile. "You'll have to help. I don't know anything about stripping furniture."

"Neither do I."

Stunned, she stared up at him. "Are you

A faint smile tugged at his lips. "Very."

"But you put it on. You should know how to off."

He shrugged. "It sounds logical when you say it, but the reality is that I have never stripped a piece of furniture in my life. I have occasionally used a blow torch to melt paint off certain things."

She frowned. "I don't think that would be good for the tables."

"Probably not," he agreed with a wry expression.

"Okay. That's a little bit of a problem, but it's certainly not insurmountable. How hard can this be? There are directions on the cans."

"Gaby, I love your enthusiasm, but we can't do this now. I have work to do downstairs. I want to get another apartment rented by the first of the month."

"Can't you leave it just for tonight?" she said, unable to hide her disappointment. "You worked all day. What kind of boss do you have?"

She watched in astonishment as he burst into laughter. "The best, actually. I work for myself."

"Well, I know you're a carpenter, for heaven's sake. And you paint. And who knows what all, but you do take jobs."

"Of course," he said. "That's where I was all day. I'm in the middle of the renovations on a house in Brooklyn Heights."

She absorbed that news. It didn't conflict dramatically with anything she'd said. "Then this is a second job?"

"This?"

"Here. Managing this building and fixing it up."

He shook his head and said with the sort of patience usually reserved for overly inquisitive children, "No, Gaby. I own this building."

She stared at him blankly, trying to absorb the implications. "But..."

"But what?"

"I thought you were just a..." Now that she knew differently, she couldn't bring herself to say exactly what she had thought.

"Don't blame me, if you jumped to a conclusion."

"You let me do it," she accused, feeling a curious mixture of betrayal and pleased astonishment. "You let me go on thinking that you were just some sort of common laborer."

The words slipped out before she had time to censor them. She recognized the mistake the instant she looked into Paul's eyes. The blue sparked with fury.

"I beg your pardon," he said with an iciness that froze her straight to the marrow in her bones. "There is nothing *common* about giving a good day's work for a good day's wages, no matter how *lowly* some people might consider the task."

"I didn't mean that," she said miserably.

"I can't see any other interpretation. When you thought I was no more than a *common laborer*," he said, apparently determined to humiliate her by throwing her own ill-considered words back in her face, "was that what kept you out of my bed? Does everything change now that you know I own property and have a bank account that doesn't provide for frills, but keeps a roof over my head? Does it, Gaby?"

She stood up and met his furious glare evenly. "I'm sorry. I'm sure it must seem that I'm the worst sort of snob, but you're deliberately misunderstanding."

His gaze was unrelenting. "Am I really? What's held you back then?"

"Because we're not right for each other," she said, knowing the argument sounded weak. There were literally hundreds of reasons two people might not be right for each other. She hadn't given him one of them.

"I'm not good enough, isn't that what you mean?"

"No," she protested, but deep inside she knew that was exactly what she'd thought.

He ran his hand through his hair. "For God's sake, Gaby, don't lie about it. What's the point?"

The point was that she didn't want him to know how shallow she was capable of being. Unfortunately it seemed he already knew it. "You knew what I thought all along, didn't you?" she said finally. When he didn't answer, she raised her voice, needing to share the anger and the blame. "Didn't you?"

He sighed wearily. "Yes. At least I suspected it."

"Then why didn't you correct the mistake then? Why did you let it come to this? Did you enjoy making a fool of me?"

"I'm not the one who did that. You did it all by yourself. You used superficial values to judge me, label me and tuck me away." He grabbed her arms and held on so tightly that she had to bite back a gasp. She refused to admit to the pain, which she was certain was no greater than the anguish she saw in his eyes.

"I'm a man, Gaby. An individual who has a thousand different facets to his personality, just like you do." Their gazes clashed, hers repentant, his blazing with anger and frustration.

"Dammit," he swore softly, his hands dropping to his side. He seemed to be biting back something, restraining himself.

Gabrielle rubbed her arms and waited for the explosion to go on. When it didn't, she said, "You might as well go on."

"No."

"Don't stop now. You're on a roll. Then, again, maybe I should remind you of the niche you've put me in and exactly how many times I've proven you to be mistaken. Don't tell me you didn't expect to have a rich prima donna, a real spoiled brat on your hands. You have a real hang-up when it comes to money. Even I can see that."

He sighed. "Okay, you're not the only villain in this piece. That's all the more reason we should stay as far away from each other as we can get. We seem to bring out the worst in each other."

Gaby refused to let that lie go unanswered. "Not always." At his shocked and disbelieving look, she added, "At least not for me."

"What are you saying?"

"All day today I've been remembering the way I felt this morning. You never even touched me and yet I felt as though I were the most desirable woman on the face of the earth. I felt a fire inside that I'd never felt before."

"That's lust, Gaby. We've never even tried to deny that we feel that. I ought to know. I came damned close to forcing myself on you in there this morning."

She shook her head and smiled. "Don't even try to turn what nearly happened here today into some sort of ugly scenario with me as the poor victim. I wanted you, just as much as you wanted me."

"It's not enough, Gaby. For this to work, we need mutual respect and we've just established that it doesn't exist. Our bodies may be in perfect harmony," he said, a bitter note of regret in his voice, "but our heads are in different worlds."

Gabrielle wanted to protest, but there was far too much truth in what he said. If they were to find their way to something real and meaningful between them, they would have to start over. The prospect might have seemed insurmountable were it not for one thing.

"What about our hearts?" she responded finally, reaching out to touch his chest. He trembled as her fingers lingered over the spot where his heart thundered at a revealing pace. "What about those?"

Paul's eyes widened at the softly spoken taunt, but she didn't wait around for an answer. She picked up her coat and left, not sure where she was going, only certain that she wanted to be far from here when she began to cry.

Seven

Paul stared at the door as it slammed behind Gabrielle, instinctively noting that the frame seemed a little loose on top. He automatically went for his hammer and a handful of nails as he pondered her exit line.

What the hell was she talking about? Had she been trying to suggest that this thing between them amounted to love? That was crazy. They barely knew each other. In fact, until tonight they'd both apparently been influenced—subconsciously at least—by fairly negative first impressions, the kind that did not inspire love or anything remotely akin to it.

Then, again, maybe that's what someone of Gabrielle's background had to think in order to justify a sexual relationship. Which, he noted ruefully, they didn't even have. Perhaps in her circles, she even had to justify desire.

Well, she could call it anything she liked. Personally, he thought lust or chemistry was a pretty adequate label. It was possible to lust after a total stranger—a lady with a pair of shapely legs, for instance, or one with long red hair that flashed fire in the sunlight. But you sure as hell couldn't love someone you didn't even know. If tonight's argument had told him anything, it was that he and Gabrielle knew as much about each other as two people who happened to sit on neighboring bar stools. They'd both been talking for days, but obviously neither of them had been listening.

And that, he decided, was something he couldn't do a damn thing about until she came home. He went back down to work on the third floor apartment. The sooner it was finished and rented, the sooner he could complete the second floor unit and then, finally, his own on the ground floor. Then there would be some space between him and Gabrielle, assuming she hadn't already moved on long before that. That prospect wasn't something he cared to think about at all.

At first, tonight, seeing the excitement that lit her eyes when she'd come in, his stomach had knotted. He'd been convinced that only a new job would spark that high-voltage smile and guileless enthusiasm. When he'd seen the two tables and realized that, for the moment, she intended to stay—job or no job—he'd been overwhelmed by relief and a vague sense of victory. It was as if those tables represented a sort of commitment.

It made what had happened afterward all the more confusing. How, in the midst of the teasing and laughter over those tables, had things gotten so intense and so wildly out of control? One minute they'd been talking about paint, putting it on and taking it off. It certainly should have been less volatile than a similar discussion about clothes, for instance. Still, the next minute accusations and countercharges were whizzing through the air aimed at hurting.

No matter how hard he tried, he couldn't account for Gabrielle's motives. To be honest, though, he understood his own all too well. In part at least, he'd been releasing years of pent-up emotions, blaming her for long-ago slights, protecting himself from the pain of another rejection. He'd set out to achieve emotional distance at a time when physical space wasn't possible. What had almost happened this morning had shown him the need for that.

Gabrielle had been gone nearly an hour when he heard the downstairs door open, then the heavy tread of slow, tired footsteps. He held his breath as the steps approached the third floor, then went on. He sighed. Apparently there would be no confrontation again tonight, no resolution of the earlier argument. Maybe it was for the best. Perhaps in the morning, with clearer heads, they could get at the real problems between them. He felt slightly guilty over his relief at the reprieve.

Working with renewed concentration on the new kitchen cabinets, he was startled when he turned and found Gabrielle standing in the doorway. She'd changed out of her tailored-for-success business suit into jeans and a surprisingly faded sweatshirt that dipped unevenly at the neckline and bagged everywhere else. She'd never looked sexier or more approachable. If he kept looking at her, it would shatter his control. He turned back to the cabinet, fitting a corner together with careful precision, then tapping a nail into place.

"What happened here tonight?" she said softly. The uncertainty in her voice was enough to tie his gut into knots all over again. He couldn't look at her. If he did, if he saw the slightest hint of vulnerability in her eyes, he would take her in his arms and they would both be lost.

"We both found out we'd been living in a dreamworld. Reality set it." He kept his voice deliberately cool, determinedly nonchalant.

"I don't think so." The crisp note of conviction surprised him.

"So what do you think happened?"

"I think we were getting too close. I think you were feeling things you didn't want to feel and you set out to destroy those feelings."

His head snapped around at that. He hadn't credited her with mind-reading and wasn't about to admit to her skill. "Where the hell would you get an idea like that?"

She was not the least bit intimidated by his gruff tone. "It's the only thing that makes sense. You admitted that you'd known all along that I had doubts about getting involved with you, so all that garbage about my being a snob was hardly news. You used it, though. You took something we hadn't even put to the test..."

"Your attitude..."

"Was based on a misperception."

"Does that make it any less unconscionable?"

"Oh, for heaven's sake, you're every bit as hung up on the class distinction as you accuse me of being. Is being a reverse snob one bit better than being a snob? I resent that label, anyway. It's not the money itself or the lack of it that creates incompatibility. Even two rich people often develop even more dramatically different life-styles, make far different choices because of the restrictions or size of their bank account."

"You went to Harvard. I went to the school of hard knocks. Is that what you mean?"

She grinned. "In a way."

"That's a wide chasm to bridge."

"Maybe."

"I tried it once before and it didn't work," he admitted, surprising himself with his candor. He'd never told anyone about Christine. His parents had guessed, of course. They had even tried to warn him the relationship was a mistake. He'd ignored the warnings.

"Why didn't it work?" Gabrielle asked.

"She was rich. I was poor."

"Was it really that simple?"

He thought about Christine, really thought about her for the first time in years. Nothing about her had been simple.

"She liked to be where the action was. If her friends were skiing in Switzerland, that's where she wanted to be. If they were on a cruise in the Mediterranean, she couldn't wait to join them. She went to every charity ball in the city, every club opening, every major art exhibit. It all cost money and I didn't have it. The few times I went with her it was a disaster. She and her crowd talked about places and people I'd never even heard of. At first I was a curiosity. But it didn't take long for her to figure out that the novelty had worn off and I didn't fit in."

"So she dumped you?"

"Something like that," he said. It was a calm, unemotional description of something that had once been devastating. Even now he couldn't recall it without a surge of anger and humiliation.

"Were you really that happy with someone so different?" He tried remembering exactly how it had been ten years ago on the day when he'd had to admit it was over. He and Christine had spent the weekend sailing with her friends in Newport. Lulled by the sun and the ever-present pitcher of vodka and tonic, he'd felt oddly detached. He'd listened to the gossip that substituted for meaningful conversation. He'd watched Christine spend an entire day worrying about her tan line. And he had been incredibly bored. Still, that night he had been caught up in years of powerful feelings again. He had proposed. What a mistake it would have been if she'd said yes.

Suddenly he grinned at Gabrielle. "That's amazing. I just realized that I was bored to tears. For ten years I've been hating myself for not being able to fit in, only to discover I'd hate being like that crowd."

"Does that mean we can put my family background aside from now on?" Before he could answer, her gaze clashed with his. He read the challenge that was in her eyes long before it crossed her lips. "Do you want me, Paul?"

He'd thought he'd prepared himself for anything, but he was stunned by the direct question. His body responded before he could begin to find the right words for an answer.

"Yes," he said finally.

"And I want you."

"Which doesn't resolve the real problem," he reminded her, ignoring the sudden tightness of his jeans across his abdomen. "Come here."

She stepped into the room. He hesitated, then put his hands around her waist and lifted her up to sit on a completed section of the counter. He stepped between her splayed knees, his hands sliding down to rest on her thighs. It took everything in his power to leave the contact between them at that.

"Gaby, what you just said makes a lot of sense. Just because your family has money doesn't mean you're at all like Christine. But you are the kind of woman who's bound to have certain expectations in a relationship. I can't promise you anything right now. I'm just beginning to get on my feet financially. My goals aren't extravagant or earthshaking, but I don't want to lose sight of them. It took me a long time to become comfortable with who I am. Now that I am, I don't want to start dreaming impossible dreams."

"Am I an impossible dream?" she said quietly, her clear eyes meeting his, then becoming shadowed by doubts. Her gaze dropped to his chest.

"Right now, yes." When she tried to interrupt, he said, "I know you're not the same shallow person Christine was. But you *are* confused and vulnerable. You're searching for answers for yourself and your future. If we become involved now, you could stop looking. Remember that Robert Frost poem about the road not taken?"

Surprise flickered in her eyes. Then she nodded.

"It was all about choices, Gaby. Unless I'm very much mistaken, tonight you don't think you have any and it terrifies you. Gabrielle Clayton has probably always had the world at her feet. She could choose any direction for her life and with a snap of her fingers, it was hers. You're facing now what I faced years ago. You can set almost any goal in life you want, you can work like hell to attain it, you can even have money and power behind you, but there are absolutely no guarantees of success. The satisfaction has to come in making the effort." He sighed, wondering if he was only talking in circles. "Am I making any sense?"

"Too much," she said with weary resignation. "I'm just not sure what it has to do with us."

He searched for the right words. He wanted her to understand that his decision was for now, but perhaps not for always. No guarantees, though. No commitment. And only a suggestion of hope.

"When—if—you and I get together, I want it to be because you have options again. I want you to feel strong and in control of your life, to know every road that's open to you. And then, if you choose to be with me, it will be because we both know it's what you want and not the desperate act of a woman who's afraid to be alone."

She listened thoughtfully, but frowned at the end. "I am not desperate," she said heatedly.

He grinned at the sign of renewed spirit. "Good. Then you won't mind waiting a while, until we both know exactly what we want."

"I'll mind," she said. "But you're right. Waiting makes a lot more sense."

Just to make sure he diminished temptation, he changed the subject. Something had put her into this strange mood tonight and he needed to understand what it was. "Want to tell me what happened on those job interviews today?"

She met his gaze, then looked away. "Not particularly."

He pressed the issue. "Were they that discouraging? Had they already hired someone?"

"No."

"Then maybe they'll call tomorrow."

She shrugged indifferently. "Maybe."

Puzzled, he probed for an explanation for her negativity. It was totally out of character for a woman who was normally optimistic, direct and determined. She had not made that climb on Wall Street by accepting defeat so readily. "Didn't you like what they were offering?"

"It wasn't that," she admitted with obvious reluctance. "In fact, the jobs were fine. So were the benefits packages."

"What about the people?"

"They were okay, I guess."

"What then?"

"I'm not sure I handled myself that well in the interviews. I just couldn't get it together somehow."

"Why?" He watched the blush creep into her cheeks and felt a pang of guilt. "It wasn't because of what happened this morning, was it?" The shade of pink deepened to rose. "Oh, Gaby, I'm sorry."

She gave him a faint smile, obviously meant to reassure. "Don't worry about it. At first I blamed it on being distracted by that, too, but I think it was more than that."

"What?"

She hesitated a long time before answering, staring at the floor when she finally did. "I think I was bored by it all." She glanced up, her expression filled with astonishment at the admission. "Can you imagine? I fought like hell to get to New York, to make it on Wall Street, then I come to one little hurdle in my career and I'm suddenly bored. Do you suppose I'm trying to find an excuse for failing?"

"Nope," he said with certainty. "I've suspected for some time now that the enchantment was past. With your drive, you'd have found another Wall Street job by now, if you'd really been looking. Besides, I don't think you're the kind of lady who needs excuses. I think you've come to a turning point. Instead of being down, you should be excited."

"Right. I have exactly fourteen hundred dollars left in my bank account, no job prospects in sight and credit card bills coming in every day. I'm thrilled."

"Focus on the good side. You're opening yourself up to new possibilities. Take something temporary, if you feel you have to. Borrow from your parents."

"Never," she said adamantly.

"Why not?" he said, struck by the fire in her quick response. "Wouldn't they give you a loan?"

"Sure. With strings."

"Such as?"

"Move home to Charleston, take up my rightful place in society, pour tea until my wrist aches, marry someone with exactly the right pedigree no matter how boring and start the cycle all over again in a new house." She shuddered. "No way."

He grinned and applauded.

"What was that for?"

"You've made your first choice."

"I made that one when I left," she said, dismissing it as any sort of big deal.

"Times change. The stakes change. The choice you made tonight is not the same one you made when you left for New York. Give yourself a little credit."

He wanted to kiss away the doubts, but knew it would be sheer folly to risk touching her at all. He'd been entirely noble for the last half hour. He'd meant every word he'd said about giving her time to find her way. But he'd realized something about himself along the way. He wanted Gabrielle Clayton in his life far more than he'd admitted up to now. He'd simply been afraid to acknowledge the feelings that were growing in him. And, despite all his talk about freedom of choice, he was going to do everything in his power to see that she stayed right here.

Everything short of seduction, he amended. For now. Which meant he had to get her out of this room at once.

"Go," he said, his voice suddenly husky. "Get some sleep."

"Can't I help? I'm lousy with a hammer, but I could paint or something."

The offer tempted, not because it would speed the work, but because it would keep her close. His noble intentions weren't etched deeply enough for that. "Not tonight. It's late. If you want to do some work in here tomorrow, I'll bring the paint down for you."

To his amazement, she actually seemed excited at the prospect. She dropped down off the counter, then gave him a quick peck on the cheek before starting from the kitchen. In the doorway, she paused and looked back. "Thanks for the pep talk."

"No problem."

"You realize, of course, that you're shattering another stereotype."

"What's that?"

"The ruthless, unsympathetic landlord."

"Wait until you miss your first rent payment," he said with mock ferocity, enjoying the burst of laughter that lingered long after she'd gone upstairs.

Over the next few weeks Gabrielle came to accept that her life was changing dramatically. She hadn't reached a decision about what sort of job to look for, but Paul had given her a short-term alternative. He'd offered her free rent in exchange for helping him with the painting in the remaining apartments. She'd protested the exchange, but he'd shown her figures to prove that he was getting the better part of the bargain.

The arrangement had a couple of side benefits, as well. She had time to continue haunting secondhand shops and fabric stores to complete the work on their place. And she got to spend time with Paul. They were together every evening, sharing sandwiches or homemade soup and, occasionally, pizza or Chinese takeout. Each day she learned something new about him, something that made her respect grow and her desire mount.

The fact that he pointedly kept his distance only escalated the heated longing that assailed her at the oddest moments. Her gaze would linger on his fingers as they clasped a wrench and her imagination would soar. She'd wipe a speck of paint from his cheek and her flesh would burn. Her body was in a constant state of repressed excitement but her thoughts were, surprisingly, calmer and more serene than she'd imagined possible.

On the day she finally finished the work on their apartment, she planned a surprise celebration. She'd even calculated the effect a bottle of wine might have on their wavering resolve. It was obvious that for the past week it had been difficult for Paul to say goodnight and go off to his own room. One night neither of them had gotten any sleep because neither would make the first move to break off the conversation that was punctuated by laughter and increasingly heavy-lidded looks of longing.

Gabrielle set the refinished oak dining room table with her best china and crystal. She polished her silver candlesticks and added a small bouquet of the last flowers from the dying garden. She'd capitulated to Paul's secret passion for thick, rare steaks and bought two of the best the butcher had. She'd made her own dressing for the salad and snapped fresh green beans. She had even made an apple pie. From scratch. She'd spent the whole afternoon peeling apples and rolling the dough for the double crust. Still warm, it was sitting on the kitchen counter now, the tempting cinnamon scent wafting through the apartment.

After her bath, she dressed in wool slacks and a soft sweater with a cowl neckline. She brushed her hair until it shone with warm golden highlights, then added a light touch of makeup.

At dusk, her anticipation mounting, she lit a fire in the fireplace and sat down to wait. As the room darkened, her spirits sank. Worry replaced excitement, followed by indignation, then deepening concern, then fury. It was after midnight when he finally arrived.

Paul took in the spoiled dinner and Gabrielle's scowl at a single glance. She bit her lip to keep from shouting at him like a fishwife. She would be calm. She would be reasonable. She would listen. And then she would heap guilt on him until he was drowning in it.

"What happened? Your date didn't show?" he said.

The man actually seemed to feel sorry for her. Either he was incredibly obtuse or he was a master at acting the innocent.

"Something like that," she said coolly, very proud of her control. "Where have you been?"

"I had dinner with a friend."

"I see." She couldn't keep the edge out of her voice, though she'd sworn at least a dozen times during the evening that she wouldn't give him the satisfaction of knowing that he'd hurt her.

He sat down in the chair opposite her, looking perplexed. "I have the feeling I'm missing something here. Are you mad at me?"

She stared at him, then shook her head. "Paul Reed, you cannot possibly be that dumb." So much for staying cool. "I spent thirty dollars on steaks and wine," she snapped. "You bet your life I'm mad at you."

He picked up the half-empty cabernet sauvignon bottle. "Apparently the wine didn't go to waste."

"Don't change the subject."

"I wasn't aware that's what I was doing."

"Couldn't you have called?"

Paul sighed. He'd stayed out on purpose tonight because it was getting so he couldn't bear being in the same room with Gabrielle and keeping his hands off her. He wanted to explore the satin texture of her skin, to set her flesh on fire. He wanted those velvet brown eyes to smolder with the heat of his touch. If he'd had any idea she was sitting in front of a fire waiting for him with wine and food, he'd probably have stayed out the rest of the night. His good intentions had withstood about all the temptation they could handle. Even now his fingers trembled from his effort at restraint. He wanted badly to caress the lines of tension on her face until they eased.

He sighed again and closed his eyes. When he opened them, he said, "Okay. I guess we'd better talk this out."

"Please, don't do me any favors," she said sarcastically. He winced under the direct hit.

"I'm sorry if you went to all this trouble for me, but you didn't mention you were going to do it," he said reasonably.

She shot him a look of pure disgust. "It was supposed to be a surprise. You've come home every night since I've been here. You have been downstairs hammering or sawing or painting by no later than five-thirty. You've stayed at it until midnight. How was I supposed to know that tonight would be the one night in a month you'd find something better to do?"

Paul couldn't think of a single adequate response for her logic. Feeling a nagging hunch that he was playing dirty, he tried putting her on the defensive. "We're roommates, Gaby. We both agreed it was for the best right now. I shouldn't have to check in with you.''

She stared at him, absorbing the low blow. "I'm not crazy about the definition of our relationship, but don't even roommates deserve consideration?''

Her chin was tilted defiantly, but there were huge tears clinging to the corners of her eyes. She looked so forlorn that he muttered a curse and went to her. Overcome with guilt, he took her chin in his hand and met her gaze.

"Of course they do. And I am very sorry I spoiled your evening.''

Suddenly her bottom lip quivered and one tear rolled freely down her cheek. Paul thought he could bear anything but her crying, especially when he felt responsible for her pain.

To prevent a second tear from following the first and then a third and on and on until his own heart broke, a kiss seemed to be the only answer. He seized it far too readily.

Just one, he promised himself as his mouth claimed hers, slowly savoring the touch of velvet against fire.

Just a fleeting taste of her lips, he vowed again, his tongue discovering the salt of tears and the tang of wine.

Just a brief offering of warmth and tenderness and understanding. Just to keep her from crying. Just between friends.

Of course, it wasn't enough.

Eight

___

For a man who was all hard angles and gruffness, Paul seduced with surprising gentleness, Gabrielle decided as he kissed away her tears. She wasn't sure what she'd expected, but it hadn't been these slow, tender caresses that melted every last bit of icy anger and left her gasping for more. The persuasive, eager touch of his lips, so long in coming, was like a taste of heaven. She wanted to linger there forever, surrounded by this astonishing sense of contentment.

"Gaby," he murmured, breaking away far too soon, just when she was getting used to the sensuous warmth of his mouth. "We can't do this."

"We can," she said, pressing her mouth against his to assure his silence. Her tongue declared a daring assault on his firmly closed lips, until they parted on a groan of pure pleasure. Desire welled inside her, filling her with an aching sense of need. The faint scent of sawdust and paint and masculinity seduced as effectively as any heady man's cologne of musk or spice. This powerful attraction between them was no longer something to talk about or even think about. It was time to feel, to let their emotions lead them for once.

Though Gabrielle had never been more certain about her own desires, more ready to listen to her heart, Paul fought this latest kiss. Her own senses heightened, she recognized his struggle to do the right thing in the tense set of his shoulders, his rigid stance. The marines would have approved of that stance. She could imagine the desperate, rational argument being waged in his head as his skin burned beneath her touch. That kind of determined logic required bold tactics. A shudder swept through him as she slid her hands beneath his shirt.

"Gaby, no." This time the protest was breathless and far less emphatic.

She lifted her confident gaze to meet his troubled expression and smiled. "Yes."

"You've had the better part of a bottle of wine. You don't know what you're doing."

She experimented with proving otherwise. She pressed her body closer to his, trailing kisses along the side of his neck, then running her tongue along the shell of his ear. A soft but distinct moan of pleasure rumbled deep in his throat. She grinned in satisfaction. "Oh, really?" she said demurely.

He scowled at her. "I was not referring to your technique."

"That's nice," she said, beginning to unbutton his shirt. Now that she was getting the hang of this, she was thoroughly enjoying it. He grabbed her hands.

"Gaby! Enough!"

She stared into eyes that glittered dangerously. "Okay."

He regarded her suspiciously, then nodded and released her. Her gaze never left his as she reached out and ran one finger lazily along the zipper of his jeans. After his first startled gasp, his jaw clenched and he swallowed convulsively. The determined look in his eyes wavered. His body's response beneath her daring touch was unmistakable.

"Damn you," he said softly, his breathing shallow.

"You don't mean that," she said, refusing to back away. Her confidence surged more powerfully than it had in weeks.

Finally Paul's hard, unblinking expression softened to one of wry acceptance. "No. I don't mean it," he said, his arms pulling her close. She could feel the ragged whisper of his breath across the top of her head.

"I don't want this to be a mistake," he said.

"It isn't," she said with astonishing certainty. If anything, Paul's doubts and restraint had proved that to her. He respected her and that was every bit as important as loving her.

She had yet to define her own feelings clearly, but she recognized that they were stronger and more powerful than anything she'd known before, a blend of friendship and desire that might very well become love. But the relationship needed intimacy to grow, to mature into something lasting. Whatever happened in the future, tonight's risk was one that had to be taken.

His hands cupped her face, the pads of his thumbs playing across her lips as he studied her intently. Gabrielle felt her heart thundering against her ribs as she waited. Finally he nodded, then lowered his mouth to hers again in a gentle promise.

When the kiss ended, he kept the promise, scooping her into his arms and carrying her through the darkened apartment to her room. He reached for the light switch, but she shook her head.

"There's a candle."

When he'd lowered her to the bed, he lit the candle, filling the room with the scent of lavender. Then he turned and started for the door.

"Paul?"

"I have to protect you. I'll be back," he promised.

Her heart filled to overflowing at this further evidence of his caring. Her trust was not misplaced. This was right. As she waited for his return, her stomach muscles tensed in anticipation of his joining her on the bed. Her pulse was beating to a sensual cadence. Then, as the narrow mattress sank beneath his weight, her skin tingled at the brush of denim and flannel against her flesh.

Expecting no more than urgency and a swift claiming from this first time together, Gabrielle instead found herself caught up in a slow building of passion. Paul teased and tempted and explored, waiting for sensation to subside before finding new ways to drive her wild with desire. She'd never imagined this exquisite tension, the urgent need to reach a peak of pleasure beyond all experience. He played her body as expertly as a longtime lover, but with the reverence of a man receiving an incredible gift for the first time. He lingered and tasted and stroked until fire consumed any remaining doubts for either of them.

His skin became slick beneath her anxious touch. His muscles tensed to steel as he moved to claim her at last. There was one unbearably slow thrust that startled her with its promise of yet more pleasure. She gasped as he withdrew, then began to fill her once again.

She heard his faint, startled exclamation of her name as if from very far away, then sensed that he was hesitating. Her body protested at the delay. Instinctively her legs circled his back and her hips rose in search of a heat that ignited her own passion.

She was vaguely aware of Paul's anguished moan as he plunged into her again. There was an instant of pain that took her by surprise and then was gone as their bodies adapted to a natural rhythm as old as time. Just when she thought she'd reached the highest peak of excitement possible, he led her on, flames of pure sensation firing her blood. And when passion exploded through her body at last, joy radiated through her heart at the unexpected sense of fulfillment.

The delicious tension slowly subsided. She opened her eyes to find Paul staring at her. "Okay?" he said, brushing damp tendrils of hair back from her face.

"More than okay." Rapture lingered as an incredible sensation of well-being.

"Why didn't you tell me?"

"Tell you what?" she said, rubbing her fingers across the stubble that darkened his jaw. The sandpapery, masculine texture sent shivers dancing through her.

"That you'd never been with a man before."

"Does it matter?" she said, feeling oddly defensive at a moment when she wanted to indulge herself in far sweeter memories.

He smiled. "Not in the way you're apparently thinking. I could have made it better for you, though."

"I doubt that," she said, a wry inflection in her voice.

Grinning slightly, Paul ran a finger across her lips. "Thanks for the flattery, but really, why didn't you say anything?"

"It's not exactly something you announce on a first date."

"This is not a first date. We've been living together for weeks now."

"Platonically."

"Barely," he said dryly.

She scowled at him. "If you want to get technical. But I still say this is our first date."

"At what point did it become a date and not just another night at home? When you decided to fix a fancy dinner? When I inadvertently stood you up? Or when you began to seduce me?"

He had a point, though she couldn't imagine why he felt the need to belabor this. Being a virgin at her age might be unusual, but it wasn't exactly a crime.

"Okay," she said grumpily. "Even tonight wasn't a date, which is all the more reason for me to have kept my mouth shut about my lack of experience. Why does that bother you so much? I thought men got all macho and tingly knowing that they were the first. Didn't I get it right?"

"Don't get testy. You got it very right. I was just surprised. You're a beautiful, desirable woman. I can't believe you've never had a serious relationship."

"Actually, I was engaged."

"And you never..." he began incredulously.

"If you'd met Townsend, you'd understand. It was a very formal engagement. Until I met you, I had no idea of the meaning of the word desire."

"I'm glad I was able to broaden your vocabulary."

All of a sudden there was an odd tension in his voice that puzzled her. It didn't fit with the tender aftermath of glorious lovemaking. "What's wrong?"

"Tell me the truth, Gaby. Was this just an experiment? You'd certainly gone out of your way to set the scene, right down to the candle by the bed. Did you decide it was time to discover your own sexuality and pick me because I was in the neighborhood and struck you as being an adequate stud?"

Shocked by the crude assessment of what had just happened between them, she sat up in bed, clutching the sheet across her breasts. She felt embarrassed and cold and incredibly empty inside.

"I really must not have gotten it right, if you think that," she said her voice flat. "I never said I didn't have opportunities to hop into bed with other men. I said I'd never had these feelings before." She glowered at him. "*You* inspire them. I don't know what they mean or the full ramifications of tonight, but I wanted this to happen between us because it felt right. Now I have to wonder if it wasn't an awful mistake."

Paul winced as if she'd slapped him. He reached out to touch her, but she shrugged off his hand.

"I'm sorry," he said. "I should never have said that. Maybe I said it because I was feeling guilty about my own motives. God knows I've wanted you from the very first moment you walked into this apartment. Up until now I've had sense enough to keep my hands off."

"You don't have any reason to feel guilty for taking what I offered, only for making it seem ugly and cheap." She allowed her point to sink in, then sighed. "Paul, I don't regret what happened tonight."

"That's not what you said a minute ago."

"I was furious at you a minute ago for trying to ruin something very special."

The tension seemed to drain from his body at last. She saw the spark of heat flare in his eyes and recognized it. "Maybe I should try to make it up to you," he suggested in a voice that sent fire sizzling through her veins all over again.

"Maybe you should."

When Paul woke in the morning, he was surprised to find that he was alone in Gaby's bed. During the night, he'd gotten accustomed to waking up and finding her nestled close beside him. Sometimes he had contented himself with just watching her sleep, filled with an overwhelming sense of possessiveness. More often, he'd needed to touch her, to feel the satin of her skin as it warmed beneath his fingers. And on more of those occasions than he'd dreamed possible, she had come awake to his touch, returning it with sleepy pleasure, until they'd wound up clinging together in passion yet again.

He stretched, got out of bed and without bothering to pick up his scattered clothes went in search of Gabrielle. He heard her before he found her, her voice low and edged with a note of nervousness he'd never heard before. He walked into the living room, where she was curled up in the corner of the sofa talking on the phone. She glanced up at him, her eyes widening as she took in his state of undress. He went over and dropped a light kiss on her forehead, then sat down across from her, feeling not one bit guilty about his blatant eavesdropping. He wanted to know what had put the tension in her voice and the frown on her forehead.

"Yes, Daddy. Of course, everything is all right. You don't need to worry about me."

Paul watched as she swallowed hard. A blush crept into her cheeks. "The job is going just fine."

Startled, he simply stared at her. She refused to meet his gaze.

"Of course, I know I can count on you and Mother. If there were anything wrong, I would tell you. I have to go now, Daddy. There's someone at the door. I'll talk to you again next week. No, really. I'll call. I'll give you the phone number next time. 'Bye.''

She pushed down the button to break the connection, even before she replaced the receiver. She still didn't look at him.

"What was that all about?"

"Just checking in with my parents. If I don't call once a week, they get a little crazy."

She started to get up.

"Don't leave."

She sat back down, looking guilty and thoroughly uncomfortable.

"You haven't told them about your job yet, have you?"

"You were sitting right here. You know I haven't."

"Or about where you're living?"

Her chin rose defiantly, then she sighed. "No."

"Why not?"

"They'd worry."

"It sounds to me as though they're already worried."

"If you knew my parents, you'd realize that it's a perpetual state of mind."

"Then why not tell them the truth?"

"Because they'd start pressuring me to come home. I'm not up to it."

"Are you afraid you'd give in and go?"

"Of course not."

"Then tell them. I could tell from the sound of your voice that the deception is beginning to take a toll on you. Get it out in the open. Let them know that you're doing just fine, that you're getting your life back together, making decisions about what you want to do next.''

"And how do I explain you?"

He grinned. "Now that's an interesting question."

"Dammit, I'm serious. If they find out I am living with a man, they won't wait around to find out the circumstances. My father will be up here with a shotgun."

"Is that really what you're afraid of? You don't seriously think your father will shoot me unless we traipse off to the nearest chapel."

"Cathedral," she corrected. "Senator Graham Clayton's daughter would only get married in the fanciest cathedral around, with an entourage and trappings that would make the royal weddings in England look like they were thrown by paupers."

"Senator Graham Clayton?" Paul repeated in a voice that was admittedly choked. The man's name was synonymous with conservative politics and old-fashioned family values. A shotgun would probably be too good for a man who was sitting around naked chatting with his daughter. He'd probably string him up from a tree in Central Park and not necessarily by his neck. "I think I see the problem."

A faint grin flitted across Gabrielle's face. "I thought you would."

"I still don't like the idea of your lying to him. If he finds out what's happened before you tell him yourself, it will only upset him more."

"How is he going to find out? He's too busy keeping the whole country on the straight and narrow to worry about one wayward daughter."

"What if he tries to call you at work?"

She stared at him, her expression horrified. "Oh, damn," she whispered softly.

"Obviously that's not something you'd considered. What if one of your friends up here tries to track you down by calling your family? You've pretty much dropped out of sight. It's not unthinkable that they'd assume you'd gone back to South Carolina."

"You're a real bundle of good news this morning, aren't you? Why aren't you still asleep?"

"I missed you," he said evenly. "Now stop changing the subject."

"I don't want to talk about this," she said stubbornly.

"Fine, but you'd better think about it. Delaying the inevitable is only going to make it worse."

He left her sitting on the sofa, staring out the window.

Senator Graham Clayton. He couldn't get the name out of his head as he dressed and went downstairs to finish painting the living room of the apartment that would soon be his. If last night had complicated his relationship with Gabrielle, this morning's revelation had given new meaning to the word. He might be considered a suitable addition to the family of some pleasant, middle-class politician whose name wasn't recognized beyond his own state, but he no more belonged in Senator Clayton's reportedly idyllic family than he did in Buckingham Palace.

"How many coats of paint are you going to put on that spot?" Gabrielle asked, interrupting his panicked thoughts.

He stared blankly at her, then at the wall. Sure enough he'd been running the roller over the exact same square for the last ten minutes. "I guess I wasn't paying attention."

"I hope you weren't down here panicking about the shotgun."

His expression must have given him away because she sighed heavily. "I knew it. I knew the minute you found out about my family, you'd start building your defenses right back up again. I can just hear that brain of yours clicking through all the reasons why we're unsuited and magnifying them out of all proportion."

"You have to admit the stakes are a lot higher than I'd realized."

"Stakes? The only thing at stake here is whether or not you and I care about each other. I can't speak for you, but I'm falling in love for the first time in my life."

Paul felt his heart stop then start again at a faster beat. He shook his head adamantly. "You can't do that."

"Who says?"

"I do. It won't work."

"It was working well enough a few hours ago."

"Don't remind me."

She walked toward him until they were standing practically toe to toe. He felt as though he were suffocating.

"I think I have to," she said softly, before curling her fingers into the hair at the back of his head. His scalp tingled and the sensation danced straight down to his... Oh, hell, he thought weakly as her lips claimed his with a possessiveness that captured his breath and robbed him of all sensible thoughts. For a woman who'd been relatively inexperienced twenty-four hours ago, she was catching on quickly.

Sparks danced in her eyes when she released him. "Remember that the next time you get any crazy ideas about going back to being my pal."

Paul refused to let a little thing like an unbridled libido destroy his common sense, which had been strengthening with a vengeance ever since that phone call. He had to find some way to remind Gabrielle of exactly how mismatched they were. They'd been living in isolated, idyllic harmony here for several weeks now. She hadn't been forced to face what his world was really like, how vastly different it was from her own.

"I've been thinking," he began, still sorting through possible ways of introducing her to reality. "This apartment will be finished in a few days now. Maybe we ought to show it off."

She regarded him suspiciously. "Where did that come from?"

"It's just an idea. I mean why not have a party? You can meet some of my friends. I can meet some of yours. We've worked hard to get this place in shape. It's time we celebrated.''

"Under normal circumstances, that would make perfect sense. Why do I have this feeling that there's a catch in there?''

"Because you have a suspicious nature?'' he suggested cheerfully.

"With good cause,'' she retorted. "Are you trying to prove something to me?''

"What would I be trying to prove?'' He concentrated very hard on dipping the roller into the paint, then spreading it onto a new section of the wall. He could not look into her eyes.

"That we mix like oil and water.''

He swallowed hard. "How would a party show that?'' he asked innocently. "It's just a bunch of people getting together for a good time.''

"Exactly. So don't get any crazy ideas that your friends will offend me so deeply that I'll stop wanting you or that my friends will be such snobs that your friends will hate them. In fact, I will go so far as to bet you that this will be the very best party you have ever been to.''

Paul had a feeling he'd gone about this all wrong. Gabrielle was now determined to make this stupid party work and she would do it, if she had to invite the symphony and the New York Rangers to entertain the divergent crowd. He didn't even need to wait for Senator Clayton to show up with his hanging noose. Right now, he had all the rope he needed to hang himself.

Nine

Despite her avowed self-confidence, Gabrielle felt trapped and more than a little worried. She had no choice now but to treat the upcoming party as a challenge. She knew perfectly well that Paul expected it to be a disaster, maybe even hoped it would be. She also knew that their future hinged in some twisted, obscure way on its success. While she resented having her fate tied to something so superficial, she accepted the situation, gritted her teeth and set out to prove Paul wrong.

Thankfully, being a politician's daughter had equipped her to play hostess at almost any kind of event from a Fourth of July picnic in a town square to a gala at the country club. She'd campaigned in factories and bowling alleys as readily as antebellum estates. She could make polite small talk with people she'd never seen before and would never see again, leaving each one convinced they were indelibly etched on her memory. It was easy enough to convince herself that unless Paul dragged in homicidal maniacs, she could maintain her aplomb.

In addition, planning a party for thirty people in her own home should be a piece of cake. She'd learned from a master. Her mother approached entertaining with the skill of a tactical expert in a military command post. Gabrielle knew all about guest lists and food quantities and wine selection. What she didn't know about, of course, were the tastes of Paul's friends.

It was the unknown factor, combined with the stakes, that gave all of her careful planning an edge of panic. A full week before the Saturday night party, she found herself filling a grocery cart with six different beers—imported and domestic, light and regular—because she had no idea which one Paul's friends might like. She bought pâté and little quiches at a gourmet French bakery, then in a frenzy of uncertainty added bags of potato chips and pretzels to the menu. She polished her silver, then decided to use Paul's stainless steel flatware. She went through the closet and picked out a basic designer dress suitable for any occasion, then changed her mind and dragged out comfortable jeans and a handknit sweater.

Unless she asked him a direct question, Paul virtually ignored the preparations. On Saturday his contribution was a trip to the corner for ice, which he dumped in the tub—before she'd had her bath. At her scowl of displeasure, he took it back out and stored it in the already crammed refrigerator. Later, as he returned the ice to the tub and added the assorted six packs of beer, she caught him grinning.

"What's so funny?" she asked, glowering. She was in no mood for amusement at her expense.

"You could open a bar with this variety."

"If you'd offered any suggestions, I might not have had to buy a little of everything."

"My friends will drink whatever's available. Won't yours?" he inquired.

"Go to hell."

The evening was certainly getting off to a stellar start, she thought as she put the finishing touches on a clam dip surrounded by chilled vegetables. Even the disparate guests were likely to get along better than the host and hostess. She absentmindedly snapped a carrot stick in two, then threw the pieces into the trash in disgust.

"Gaby."

"What?"

"This is not worth having a nervous breakdown over."

"Isn't it? You're hoping everyone will have a rotten time, just so you can say I told you so and move out of here with a clear conscience."

He came up close behind her and slid his arms around her waist. The fresh, tangy scent of his aftershave teased her senses. "No. I'm not."

"You are." She turned around in his embrace so she could read his expression. "And I want your friends to like me. I really do, but if they don't, it shouldn't have anything to do with what's happening between us. I'm not worried about what my friends think of you."

"Aren't you?"

"No."

"How many of your friends did you invite?"

"Okay. I only invited a few, but I don't have that many close friends here anyway. Ted and Kathy were the only couple I got really close to and Jeff was an office pal. They're the only people I've stayed in touch with. And no matter what you think, I am not a believer in the old adage that you can judge a person by the friends he keeps. People develop relationships— and marriages, for that matter—for all sorts of reasons."

"I know that," he said with a sigh.

Despite the reassuring words, the tone wasn't convincing. Gabrielle's feeling of dread returned as she turned back to the arrangement of carrot and celery sticks. Paul left to put music on the stereo.

When the first knock came at the door, she tensed and wondered exactly how long she could get away with taking refuge in the kitchen. Despite the fact that she was never more than three feet from the stove, the quiches burned because she forgot all about them as she tried to hear how things were going in the living room.

She was on the verge of tears, infuriated by her own silly retreat, when Paul returned to the kitchen for beers for the first arrivals.

"What's wrong?" he asked at once.

"I burned the quiches."

"There's enough food in there to feed all the homeless in Manhattan. Don't worry about the quiches. Just come on out."

She shook her head.

He stared at her. "Why not? I thought you were going to stop worrying about how well everyone got along and just enjoy this party. I thought you wanted to prove something to me tonight."

She glared at him. Talk about throwing down the gauntlet or hoisting her with her own petard. The man had a particularly nasty habit of throwing her words back in her face.

"Let's go," she said determinedly, aware that there was an unmistakable note of doom in her voice.

Once in the living room she noticed that people actually seemed to be enjoying themselves. Jeff Lyons, who was handsome, funny and gay, was discussing racketball with one of Paul's friends. Ted and Kathy waved from across the room, where they were talking to a young blond man she recognized as a member of Paul's work crew. A beautiful woman with spiky black hair and a studded leather jacket over her denim miniskirt was enthusiastically describing her latest art exhibit to a rapt woman in a Norma Kamali original. Since Gabrielle didn't recognize either one of them, she assumed they were both friends of Paul's. Apparently his own social circle contained an eclectic mix.

So, she thought with the first flicker of relief, it wasn't going to be so awful. People weren't sorting themselves out into his friends and hers with an obvious chasm in between. Maybe she'd been right all along. She allowed herself a small, triumphant smirk before going to introduce herself to the artist. She seemed like a likely person to begin with. They would at least have art in common.

She had barely given her name when the artist's heavily made-up dark brown eyes widened to the size of a Kewpie doll's. "So you are the one. I'm so glad to finally meet you. I'm Theresa. Paul tells me he brought you to see some of my work."

An unfortunate image of auto parts entwined with clocks came to mind. Tongue-tied with astonishment, Gabrielle stared at her. "Yes," she said finally. "It was..."

Theresa laughed. "Don't bother trying to be polite. My work falls into that love it or hate it category. Maybe if I did something a little more mainstream, I wouldn't be broke all the time." She shrugged indifferently. "What's money, though, as long as I have my artistic integrity intact?"

"Money pays the bills," the owner of the Norma Kamali outfit said. "Maybe you should just marry wealth the way I did. I can paint what I want without worrying about critical or popular success."

"Don't pay any attention to all that cynical talk," Theresa said. "Maureen is also crazy in love with the man in spite of his millions and her work is now selling for $2500 a canvas. By the way, Gabrielle, Paul was telling us you're responsible for the decor in here. It's fantastic. You have a real eye for color and proportion."

Gabrielle tried to survey the room with an objective eye. It was better than before, but hardly the stuff of an interior designer's dreams.

"I'm glad you like it," she said cautiously, wondering how much simple politeness had contributed to the compliment.

"I do. Did it cost a fortune? I know I'm being terribly nosy, but when you've lived in a dump like mine, this looks wonderful. I'd give anything to have my place fixed up like this, but most of my money goes right back into art supplies."

"Actually, I did this on half a shoestring."

Maureen looked surprisingly impressed. "How? I just paid a fortune to an interior designer and the results aren't half as interesting. My apartment looks exactly like twenty others on the Upper West Side."

Basking in the apparent enthusiasm, Gabrielle described her forays through the secondhand stores and fabric shops. "Actually, it was fun. I refinished the furniture myself. It's not exactly professional caliber work, but there's a sense of adventure in discovering what's under all the grime."

"It looks great to me," Theresa said enthusiastically. "I don't suppose you'd like to take on a client. You'd have to work with a pretty limited budget and we'd have to negotiate your commission, but I'd love to see what you could do with my place."

The idea intrigued her. "What exactly would you need to have done?"

"Everything," Maureen said fervently before Theresa could respond. "How an artist can live in that dreary place is beyond me. I'd be painting in black and gray. Come to think of it maybe that does explain your sculpture."

"Very funny. As you can see, Gabrielle, I do need help. Paul volunteered to come over sometime and help me paint, but I haven't even had time to pick out a color scheme."

"Thank God," Maureen said. "Her idea of subtlety is purple and orange."

Gabrielle laughed. "I suppose I could take a look at your place and see if I get any ideas. I wouldn't want to charge you for it, though. I have some time right now and I enjoy digging around for bargains."

"Oh, no," Theresa said. "This is business. Don't sell yourself short. Turning an empty space into a warm, inviting home is a talent. I insist on paying you for it."

Just then Jeff came over. She introduced him to the two women, then after a promise to call Theresa about the decorating, she began circulating, checking the food, greeting newcomers. She finally made her way to Paul, who was chatting enthusiastically with Ted and Kathy. To her surprise they were discussing the construction of the apartments. Ted was amazingly knowledgeable.

"I was just telling Paul that Kathy and I have been looking for a place just this size," Ted said, after giving her a kiss. "We want to move before the baby comes."

"But you have a wonderful apartment," she protested. Paul's arm settled around her shoulders. She was surprised at how right the gesture felt and how casually Paul had made it. Perhaps he was beginning to relax with the success of the evening, too. She glanced at Ted, trying to judge his reaction, but he seemed far more interested in examining the quality of the woodwork.

"A wonderful, expensive, small apartment," Kathy corrected, rubbing her hand over her expanding belly. "It's not big enough for us *and* the baby. I'm not going to be working for at least a few months after the baby is born and with the market slow right now, we don't want to get in over our heads financially."

"You could rent one of these, if you're interested," Paul said. Gabrielle stared at him in astonishment. The second and third floor were already rented. The tenants were moving in December first. The only empty apartment was Paul's on the ground floor. He'd intended to move in next week. They hadn't discussed what their living arrangements would be after that. This was the first indication she'd had that Paul was actually thinking that they should continue living together.

"I could show you the one that's available," he offered now.

Kathy's eyes lit up. "I'd love to see it."

"But don't you think it's a little too far out?" Gabrielle said, still feeling that a move that had turned out to be so right for her might be very wrong for Ted and Kathy. "The neighborhood is still in transition. It's not what you're used to."

"But it's on the way up, not down," Ted countered. "I noticed that as we were driving over."

"But you should be thinking of buying, not pouring your money into rent," Gabrielle said, not sure exactly why she was fighting the idea of having these two lovely people as neighbors when they were clearly enthusiastic about the prospect.

"Right now all the property we like is out of our price range. I'd rather rent someplace like this for a while, so we can build our savings," Kathy said. "Ted, let's go look."

"I'll stay here," Gabrielle said, watching as Paul led them away. He and Ted were already exchanging ideas for further development of the neighborhood. Astonishing, she thought as she watched them go.

She was in the kitchen when they came back. Kathy's face was alight with excitement. "It's wonderful," she enthused. "The second bedroom will be perfect for a nursery. We're going to talk about it some more, but I think we're going to take it."

She hugged Gabrielle. "I have to get home and put this soccer kicker inside me to bed, but thank you so much for inviting us over tonight. It's been far too long since we've seen you. It would be fantastic to have you and Paul for neighbors."

"Yes," Gabrielle said, feeling numb at the speed with which events seemed to be taking place. Decisions had been made tonight she hadn't been consulted on and couldn't begin to understand.

It wasn't until all the guests had left and Paul was stretched out on the sofa that she had a chance to think about her reaction to the prospect of having Ted and Kathy living downstairs.

"Come sit with me," Paul said.

"I want to get some of this mess cleaned up."

"It can wait. I want to talk to you."

Sighing, she went to join him. He pulled her down into his lap, his arms around her waist. The increasingly familiar sense of belonging crept over her as she leaned back against his chest.

"I thought the evening went well," he said, his fingers idly stroking her stomach.

"Yes."

"Why so down, Gaby? I thought you'd be gloating. It all worked out, just the way you expected it to. I like your friends. You like mine. Nobody was standing in judgment of anyone else."

"It was all very civilized," she agreed testily.

"I thought it was better than that. People actually seemed to be having fun. Our lives are blending together."

"I suppose."

He kissed the back of her neck. "Then what's the problem?"

"How can you rent that apartment to Ted and Kathy?" she blurted finally. "It's all wrong for them."

"How do you figure that? They want two bedrooms. It has two bedrooms. They want a moderate rent. I'm asking a moderate rent. The garden even gives them a place for the baby to play."

Unexpected tears welled in her eyes. "How terrific for them," she said.

"Gaby! Don't you want them here?" He sounded confused and dismayed. "They're your friends. I thought you'd love the idea of having them nearby."

"It's not that," she said, recognizing that she was babbling incoherently, but not sure exactly what the real problem was.

"That was supposed to be your apartment," she said finally.

She heard Paul's sharp intake of breath. "I see. I didn't realize you were so anxious for me to move downstairs."

"It's not that, either."

"Are you upset because I just assumed you'd want me to stay up here with you?" he asked patiently.

"No. It's . . . it's the garden." The minute she'd said it, she felt absolutely ridiculous, but she knew it was the truth. She loved that garden. She'd been waiting for the day in the spring when it would be blooming just beyond their living room window.

"What?" Paul said, clearly baffled.

"I wanted the garden to be ours."

"It is ours."

"No. It will be theirs."

"Did you want us to move downstairs? Is that it?"

She smiled shakily. "Silly, isn't it? I guess that is what I wanted. We worked on that apartment together. I picked out the paint and the Formica for the kitchen. I sanded those floors. I thought of it as ours."

"But you worked so hard to decorate this one. I guess I thought you'd rather stay here. I can always tell Ted and Kathy that this is the one for rent."

"That's dumb. This is a perfectly wonderful apartment and you're right, we have gotten it fixed up just the way we wanted it ... except for the tub in the kitchen, that is. And Kathy shouldn't have to climb all those stairs."

"Does that mean it's okay with you, if we rent to them?"

"Yes."

His fingers stroked even more possessively across her abdomen. "I'm glad it matters to you where we live," he said softly. "But the main thing is, we're still going to be together. I have to admit that we got past a big hurdle tonight."

Yes, she thought, allowing herself to indulge in a feeling of contentment at last. That was one thing that had come out of tonight. They were together, bound more inextricably than ever.

"I had a talk with your friend Theresa," she told him. "She wants to pay me to help her decorate her place."

"That's great. Are you going to do it?"

"I thought it might be fun. At least it'll keep me busy until I finally decide what I want to do."

"Maybe this is what you should be doing with the rest of your life," he suggested slowly, as if trying to gauge her reaction. "You enjoy it. There's a need for it."

"Don't be silly. The is just a one-shot deal. It'll keep me from going crazy until I find real work."

"Maybe," he said, but there was a more hopeful look in his eyes than she'd ever seen before.

"You really think this could be the answer for me, don't you?"

"Think about it. You seemed awfully happy when you were fixing this place up. You were excited every time you discovered some treasure buried in a second-hand store. Isn't that what a career should be? Something that's fun, as well as lucrative?"

"But this is more like a hobby."

"Only because you've treated it that way. It doesn't have to be. It could be good for us, too."

She drew in a deep breath. "What do you mean?"

"It's something we could do together. It would be a natural. You could think up some jazzy little name for the business, even print up cards. When I do jobs, people are always asking me if I know anyone who does decorating for less than an arm and a leg. We could specialize in low-cost but very classy renovations."

"You might be right. It would put us on an equal footing," she said thoughtfully, unaware of Paul's sudden tension.

"Meaning?"

"It would put an end to this hang-up you have about me being better than you."

Paul pushed her aside and stood up, his expression furious. "Dammit, you just don't get it, do you?"

"What's wrong?" she asked as he paced around the room, raking his fingers through his hair.

"Can't you see that this has nothing to do with putting us on an equal footing economically? I want you to be happy. If going back to a brokerage house, putting in endless hours and developing ulcers in a quest for a six-figure income makes you happy, then go for it. My ego can stand it if you make ten times what I do. I love you, Gabrielle. I'm not trying to own you.''

Breathless and wide-eyed, she stared at him. ''You love me?''

He stopped pacing and stood gazing down at her. ''I suppose I do,'' he said as if the thought had just made itself very plain for the first time.

A soft smile began slowly, then blossomed across her face. That warm, melting feeling played havoc with her senses. ''Then why are you so far away, when you could be down here holding me?''

After a hesitation that went on so long it almost frightened her into thinking he was having second thoughts, he moved back to her side at last. She knew as his lips came down hard on hers that simply saying the words did not assure them of an easy time of it from now on, but it was a start. With their feelings out in the open, they could finally begin to make decisions about what was best not just for them as individuals, but for the two of them together. It was unlikely that they would always agree, but they were learning the art and rewards of communication and compromise.

For now, though, his mouth was hot and urgent against hers and problems that might creep up in the future were the last thing on her mind.

Ten

———

Gabrielle found that decorating Theresa's apartment was an entirely different challenge from selecting the pieces for her own place. The artist's bold personality required more vibrant colors, more unorthodox accessories. Her search for the right things led to the discovery of even more stores that stocked inexpensive used furniture, carpet remnants and even cast-off, unrestored antiques.

She came home every day exhausted, but filled with enthusiasm. Her once well-manicured nails had long since chipped and broken so badly that she had to keep them short and unpolished. She usually had tiny spatters of paint on her eyelashes or the tip of her nose. She rarely dressed in anything fancier than jeans. Her hair was usually pulled back into a simple ponytail. Her arms were constantly sore from hauling her finds home to be repaired and then to Theresa's. Equally filthy and bone-weary, she and Paul fought over the hot water in the evening, more often than not sharing the old-fashioned, oversize tub and a bottle of wine as they talked about their days. She'd never looked less sophisticated or felt a greater sense of contentment in her life.

One night Paul found her already deep in scented bubbles, the kitchen filled with a pattern of soft colors cast from a beautiful Tiffany lamp she'd spent the afternoon cleaning up.

"I like the atmosphere," he said quietly, standing in the doorway.

Her skin tingled just from the heated expression in his eyes. "Join me," she suggested.

Without taking his eyes from hers, he dropped his toolbox on the floor and began stripping off his clothes. The sheepskin jacket fell first, followed by his plaid flannel shirt. He tugged his T-shirt from the waistband of his jeans, then lifted it over his head, baring an expanse of chest matted with dark whorls of hair. Work boots were kicked off, then socks tossed aside. His fingers lingered at the snap on his jeans, his eyes filling with amusement as he teased her with a deliberate delay.

Gabrielle took a slow sip of wine and watched, her heart thumping unsteadily in her chest. Lord, the man was gorgeous. She wondered if there would ever be a day when the sight of him didn't set off sparks deep inside her. He stripped off the jeans at last, then the jockey shorts as her breathing set a pace just short of ecstasy.

He slid into the tub, his legs stretched intimately alongside hers. Pink and aqua lights danced across the bubbles.

"Where'd you find the lamp?"

"Hmm?" she murmured, reluctant to shift to a more impersonal mood.

"The lamp," he said, grinning.

She tried to tamp down her wildly vivid imagination, which was far removed from lamps. "Down near the Bowery." Her voice still had a whispery quality.

He stared at her, horrified. "Gaby, I don't want you going down there."

The delicious mood vanished at once as his sharp tone registered. "It's safe enough in the daytime," she said, then added pointedly, "it's certainly not that much worse than this neighborhood."

Her stubborn independence had become a frequent source of minor irritation to him. He was beginning to learn, though, that his objections only caused her to dig in her heels. She restrained a grin now as he reluctantly swallowed more protective advice.

"Are we keeping the lamp?" he asked finally, conceding the argument. "It doesn't look like it would fit with what you've been getting for Theresa."

"No and it doesn't really fit with what we have here, either, but the price was too good to pass up."

"Maybe that's because some of the glass is missing."

For a man who'd bought a run-down building and envisioned these wonderful apartments, he was amazingly short-sighted about potential when it came to her finds. "Obviously," she agreed. "But last week I found a woman who does work with stained glass. I think she'll give me a deal on fixing it. I'm taking it over tomorrow."

"And then what?"

"And then I'll have it in case I ever need it."

Paul grinned. "Need it for what?"

She splashed water at him with her foot. "Stop pushing. I haven't decided yet about the business."

"Haven't you?"

"Paul, there might never be another soul who wants to hire someone just to shop the secondhand stores for them."

"I have a customer now who's interested," he said nonchalantly, gazing up at the pattern of lights on the ceiling as if her response weren't of the slightest interest to him. It was one of his more infuriating methods for manipulating her.

"If you're not too busy," he added. "I've told him you're pretty booked."

Her curiosity was instantly aroused, just as he'd known it would be. She deliberately ran her foot down his chest to get his attention.

"Okay, don't stop now, you rat. Who is it? What is the place like? What kind of look is he after? What sort of budget does he have?"

He met her gaze with feigned surprise. "I take it you're interested after all."

"Don't smirk. I'll talk to him."

"Not just him, Gaby. Don't you think it's time you named this business and printed up cards? I'll bet those stores you've been patronizing would even hand them out for you."

She considered the possibility thoughtfully. The idea was beginning to intrigue her more than she'd been willing to admit. "They might," she conceded.

"Then why are you hesitating? Are you afraid of failing? You have a sound business mind. You must see that the opportunity is there, if you want it. You'd be offering a unique service. I'm sure Theresa will spread the word and I have plenty of customers who'll jump at the chance to have someone decorate for them at a reasonable cost."

"I suppose you're right, but what if I get bored with this, the way I did with Wall Street? So far it's been fun, but I've only done our place and Theresa's."

Paul captured her foot and kissed her toes. His fingers massaged away the last of the soreness and the kisses sent waves of heat spiraling through her. It was a fantastic distraction.

"Then you'll do something else," he said when she'd almost forgotten the question. "It's not as if this will require a major capital investment that will be at risk. How much can business cards cost? You don't have to worry about inventory or the overhead of office space. You don't even have to buy a fancy wardrobe. Your expenses will be at a minimum."

"My parents—"

"Have nothing to do with this decision," he said firmly. "Besides, don't they want you to be happy? They'll probably be thrilled to hear that you've started your own business."

Gabrielle had her doubts about that. They might approve of her operating a discreet, exclusive antique store in the center of old Charleston. But they would die of shame if they ever saw the rundown places she visited to find her bargains. They'd also probably hire a bodyguard to trail around after her.

But she could not live her life for her parents. She'd known that when she'd left South Carolina and it was no less true now. She finally gave free rein to the excitement that had been building inside her ever since they'd first discussed the idea. She grinned at Paul. "Let's go for it."

"I assume you're referring to the business," he said as his fingers trailed a blazing path up her leg. Her breath caught in her throat.

"That, too," she said in a voice suddenly slowed by desire.

"Want to talk about the details?" he inquired as he did something particularly magical to the back of her knee.

"Later," she murmured weakly.

"Smart woman. It's nice to know that your priorities remain in order now that you're a career woman again," he said as he lifted her from the tub and carried her down the hall. She was too busy running her tongue along the rivulets of water on his neck to reply.

* * *

Second Chances, despite certain personal distractions that occasionally took precedence, turned into a flourishing business. Paul and Gabrielle had more work than they could handle. The commissions weren't huge, but the satisfaction was tremendous and working with Paul gave her new respect for his talent at renovation. He did caring, conscientious work and his customers appreciated it.

On a personal level, their lives had meshed so completely that she couldn't imagine a future without Paul. She'd found her ideal mate, a man who was strong and supportive and caring, in the most unlikely place of all. She was still in his arms early one morning when she received a frantic phone call from Ted.

"What on earth is wrong?" she asked at once. "You're babbling. Slow down. Is it Kathy?"

"No. It's you. You're going to kill me."

The genuine panic in his voice made her very nervous. Ted was the calmest man she'd ever met. "Would you please just tell me what's wrong?"

"It's your parents."

Oh, hell. "What about my parents?"

"They're here."

Shock and dismay swept through her. "Here? In New York?"

"Yes, in New York." He took a deep breath, while Gabrielle's breath stopped. "Actually they're in this office. I got in a few minutes ago and they were already here waiting for you."

"At seven-thirty?"

"Gabrielle, you used to be in the office by seven," he reminded her. "They expected to find you here."

"What have you told them?"

"I haven't said anything yet, except that I'd try to reach you. No one else had the nerve to tell them you didn't work here anymore."

She swallowed hard. "Do you think they've figured it out?"

"Not yet, but they're beginning to guess that something's wrong. Your father's pacing and I've seen that expression before. It's the one he had on his face when he lost the vote on that health care amendment. I can't stall them much longer. They wanted me to give them your new number."

Paul had remained silent up until now, but he suddenly took the phone from her hand. "Ted, what's the problem?"

While Gabrielle pulled her knees to her chest, wrapped her arms around her legs and shivered uncontrollably, Paul extracted information from Ted. She was barely listening. This was her worst nightmare come true. She should have told her parents weeks ago. She could have sent a letter. She could have done almost anything except what she'd done, which was to hide from the truth in Brooklyn. She'd been living in a make-believe world.

She tuned back into the phone call just as Paul said, "Fine. Send them over."

"No," Gabrielle yelped, grabbing for the phone. "Ted, you can't send them here. Tell them I'll meet them at the Waldorf or the Plaza, anyplace they like in an hour. I need to explain things to them.''

''You can do that here,'' Paul said quietly.

She saw the ominous look in his eyes, the stiff set of his jaw and flinched. This was something she couldn't give in about, though. She had to see them alone. She could not expose Paul to an outpouring of their anger and dismay. She could not risk their disdain of the life she and Paul had built together. Once she'd explained, told them how well things were going for her now, how much she loved Paul, maybe it would be okay. They weren't unfeeling ogres, for heaven's sake.

Clenching the phone so tightly her hand hurt, she repeated, ''Tell them I'll meet them.''

They agreed on the Palm Court at the Plaza at nine. She hung up, more shaken than she'd ever been in her life. Not even her announcement of her plan to move to New York had terrified her like this.

''If you do it this way, we don't have a chance,'' Paul said.

''It's the only way I can do it. I have to prepare them.''

''For what? Your great come-down in life? Me?''

''I don't mean it like that,'' she said miserably.

''How do you mean it? What you're doing sounds exactly like what someone who's ashamed of her life would do.''

She looked at it through Paul's eyes and understood why he felt that way. ''Please, try to understand. I just want it to be perfect when they meet you. I'll explain everything and then I'll invite them over for dinner tonight. Is that all right?''

He nodded reluctantly. "I suppose that will have to do."

She slid her arms around his waist and rested her head against his chest. "I do love you."

He sighed heavily. "I know, Gaby. I'm just not sure it's enough."

Gabrielle walked into the Plaza with her shoulders squared and her head held high. Only she knew that an army of butterflies had been allowed to fly free in her stomach.

She saw her parents at once. Her father's steel-gray hair, florid complexion and ramrod straight posture were unmistakable. Her mother looked like an exquisite doll beside him. She was patting his hand, a familiar gesture that usually meant her father was about to explode and her mother was trying to forestall it. As she approached, her mother's face flooded with relief.

"Gabrielle, darling, here you are at last."

She bent over to give her mother a kiss. "I'm early," she said in response to the implied criticism. She felt herself regressing automatically to six-year-old status and pulled herself together.

"You know your father. He has absolutely no patience. He was furious when we got in last night and he realized we wouldn't be able to reach you until this morning. Then when you weren't at the office... Well, thank heavens, that nice young man was there."

"Ted." Gabrielle looked at her father and saw the affection in his eyes that counterpointed his scowl. She gave him a kiss. "Hi, Daddy. Why didn't you let me know you were coming?"

"How the hell were we supposed to do that?" he grumbled. "It was a last-minute thing. You know I don't approve of personal calls at work and you haven't seen fit to give us your new phone number."

"Sorry, Daddy," she said, sitting down gratefully and grabbing a menu before she could start wallowing in apologies. "Have you ordered yet? I'm starving."

"No, dear. We've been waiting for you."

"Why weren't you in the office, Gabrielle?" her father demanded. She'd wondered how long it would take for him to get to the point, but she still wasn't prepared for the question.

"You've been fired, haven't you?" he said when she didn't respond.

"Yes," she said, meeting his gaze evenly. This was it. The next few minutes would decide once and for all if she was a grown-up, independent woman or a coward.

Her mother gasped. "Darling, why didn't you tell us? We would have helped. Your father has contacts, I'm sure."

"I didn't want to use Daddy's contacts. I knew I could handle things myself."

"But what are you doing for money? That's why you moved, isn't it? You were running out of money. Oh, dear heavens, Gabrielle, you're not living in some awful place with cockroaches, are you?"

Gabrielle grinned despite herself. "No. Actually the apartment is quite nice. It's a renovated brownstone in Brooklyn."

Her mother turned pale at that. She'd barely accepted the idea of Manhattan. Brooklyn was beyond her imagination. None of her friends ever visited Brooklyn. They rarely got beyond the Plaza and Fifth Avenue.

"Is it safe?" her father demanded at once.

"Safe enough. And..." She couldn't meet their eyes. "Actually, I have a roommate."

"Another stockbroker?"

"No."

"One of your friends from school?" her mother said hopefully.

"No. It's someone I met when I first moved in." She'd gotten this far. She might as well go for the rest. "It's a man and I'm very much in love with him. He's a contractor. He does renovations."

"Oh, my," her mother said, waving her napkin to stir a breeze. She did look ready to faint. Gabrielle encouraged her to take a sip of water.

"I'm fine, dear. It's just that this is such a surprise."

"Shock would be more like it," her father growled. "Who is this man? What do you know about him? What's his family like? I hope you've looked at his background very carefully, Gabrielle. A woman in your position can't be too careful. It would be just like some con artist to take advantage of you because of me."

"Actually, Paul didn't even know you were my father until quite recently. He wasn't wild about it."

"What!" Her mother was aghast. "Why on earth not?"

"Because he's a wonderful, sensitive man. He sensed that you would disapprove of him because he's not rich and powerful. I'd like it very much if you would help me prove him wrong. I'd like you to come to dinner tonight."

"Like hell we will," her father said. "I do not condone your living with a man, no matter what his financial status, without being married. It goes against everything I stand for."

"I'm not asking for your blessing, Daddy," she said with quiet finality. "This is what I want. You can either accept it or not. It's your decision. I'll understand if you feel it would put you in an uncomfortable position politically."

"Now, Gabrielle," her mother whispered in a shocked tone, instinctively reaching out to pat her husband's hand. "Your father is worried about you, not his political career."

"Then please come tonight," she said again. "I really think you'll like Paul, if you give him a chance."

"Is he keeping you?" her father said bluntly.

Gabrielle swallowed her fury and managed to say politely, "No, Daddy. We've started a business together. I'm earning my own way."

"What kind of business could you possibly do with a contractor?"

"We'll tell you all about it tonight. Will you be there?"

Her mother cast a look of entreaty toward her father. "Please."

He sighed heavily, then said with obvious reluctance, "Okay. We'll be there."

Once the shock of her news wore off, they spent the rest of the meal catching up on other gossip from home. Gabrielle gave them her address, then went home to prepare a dinner that hopefully would soothe her father into a more receptive mood.

It might have been better, she thought later, if she'd fed him tranquilizers. From the minute her parents walked through the door, the tension was so thick it would have taken an ax to chop through it. Everyone was so incredibly polite, she felt like choking.

Her parents found her apartment *quaint*. The word was said with a slightly disdainful sniff. Paul congratulated her father on a recent victory in the Senate. She knew it was for a bill with which he violently disagreed, but he kept his own opinion in check. Her mother found Paul *charming*. That was said with a subtle lift of her eyebrows, meant to be seen only by her father. Naturally Paul saw it as well and the lines of tension around his mouth deepened. And then there were the less than subtle comments about Townsend, how devastated he was over the broken engagement, what a wonderful future he had, how often his family inquired about Gabrielle.

The final blow for Gabrielle came when they pointedly wondered when she'd be coming home to stay. It was as if they hadn't heard a single word she'd said that morning.

Shocked and infuriated by the blatant rejection of her life with Paul, she said, "I'm not coming home. I thought I'd made that clear this morning."

"But, dear, you can't go on living this way," her mother said, twisting her napkin nervously.

"What way is that, Mrs. Clayton?" Paul said.

Gabrielle heard the restrained fury in his voice and waited for the explosion. Her mother, however, hadn't been a politician's wife for thirty years for nothing.

"Paul, it's not that we don't appreciate your giving Gabrielle a place to stay," she said, immediately reducing his status to that of Good Samaritan. "Nor is it that we think your apartment isn't lovely. You've done an interesting job of fixing it up."

There was that word, Gabrielle thought with a groan. *Interesting*.

"Actually, your daughter is responsible for the decor," Paul replied with obvious pride. "She's becoming quite a success as a decorator."

Her mother looked startled. Gabrielle shot a guilty look at Paul. "I hadn't told them about the business yet."

"I see," he said heavily.

Gabrielle heard the defeat in his voice, but had no idea how to reassure him short of turning the dinner into a family shouting match. She listened to her father's patronizing remarks and her mother's weak attempts to pacify everyone and saw Paul fighting to remain calm.

"Perhaps I'd better leave," Paul said finally. "I'm sure you have things you'd like to discuss without an outsider present."

"Paul," Gabrielle protested helplessly as he grabbed his jacket and strode to the door.

"We'll talk later," he said curtly. "Good night, Mr. and Mrs. Clayton."

Gabrielle watched Paul go and knew the greatest fear she'd ever known, greater than losing her job, greater even than losing her family's support. And it made her blazing mad, at her parents and most of all at herself. Paul had chosen to act charitably and ignore her parents' rudeness, rather than fight back. She should have had the courage to defend not only him, but their relationship.

"How dare you?" she said, turning on her parents the minute Paul had left.

"What did we do?" her mother asked in seemingly genuine bewilderment.

"You've just spent most of the evening putting Paul down. Putting both of us down. Even after Paul mentioned our business, you weren't interested enough to ask about it. You've just confirmed for him what he's always feared, that he's not good enough for me." She gulped back a sob. "Well, you're wrong. He is good enough. He's better than either one of you."

Her mother gasped and her father looked more furious than she'd ever seen him.

"Young lady, you will apologize to your mother and me at once."

"I will not. You have been unforgivably rude to a man I love."

Her mother seemed to rally. "Darling, we certainly never meant to insult Paul."

"Gabrielle knows that," her father said. "The man has to understand that we're just looking out for your welfare. Now Townsend—"

"I don't want to hear one more word about Townsend," she snapped. "You say you just want the best for me. Has it occurred to either of you yet that what I have right now might be the best for me? Have you been paying any attention at all to what's been going on here tonight? I've never been happier. I love Paul. I hope to God he loves me enough to forgive your behavior. This is where my life is now, not in Charleston and certainly not with Townsend."

Her father reached for her hand. Without the bolstering effect of his anger, he looked older. To her amazement he even looked a little bit afraid. "Gabrielle, honey, your mother and I just worry about you. This isn't what we envisioned for you."

"It's not what I envisioned, either, but Paul is what's best for me. I've never been more certain of anything in my life. He's encouraged me to discover who I really am, rather than to rebel against what I don't want to be."

"What about Wall Street? You were so dead set on that once," her father reminded her.

"Maybe it was because I knew you and mother would hate it. I saw the life you had in mind for me, married to Townsend, spending my days doing dull, boring, predictable things and I reached out for the one thing that I knew was more exciting. I always envied you going off to work every day, while mother had to stay at home.''

"But I love being at home," her mother protested.

"I know you do," Gabrielle said more gently. "And I guess that's what we all need to realize. Each of us is entitled to make our own happiness, whatever it is. Mine is with Paul, with this new business of ours.''

"You really are sure about this, pet?" her father said, squeezing her hand. He searched her eyes for an answer.

"I really am."

"Then I suppose that will have to be good enough for me. We'll wait with you until Paul comes back. We'll explain that we were wrong."

One thing about her father, when he'd been convinced of something, he gave it his full-fledged support. She got up and kissed him. "Thank you, Daddy, but no. I think we'd better be alone. I'll call you in the morning. Maybe we can get together again before you leave.''

"I'd like that," her father said. "I'd like to get to know this man you love. He must be something for you to care this much.''

"He is, Daddy. He's pretty special."

Her parents left then amid more apologies and promises to be available for any plans she and Paul wanted to make with them.

Left unspoken was Gabrielle's greatest fear: that the apologies might be too late, that Paul might not come back to her at all.

Eleven

When Paul left the apartment, he walked aimlessly for a while, then got into his car. His stomach was in knots. He couldn't think straight. Only once before in his life had he felt this lost and defeated and furious. Not since he and Christine Bentley Hanford had stood under a starry sky, and she'd stared at him in astonishment as she laughed at his proposal. He had felt like such a fool. In all these years since that humiliating night, he had never felt such gut-wrenching inadequacy. He had avoided any situation, any person likely to put him at such a disadvantage again.

Until Gabrielle. Until this beautiful, vulnerable woman had come along and convinced him that what they had together could survive anything. But not this, he thought angrily. Gabrielle's parents had dismissed him as casually as they might a servant. Worse, he had tolerated it, which didn't say much for his character or for his sense of self-worth. How would Gabrielle ever respect him after this?

Without realizing where he was headed, he found himself on his way to Long Island. Maybe there were answers to be found in the past. Maybe he needed to link these two failures in his mind in order to walk away from Gabrielle with his dignity intact.

One thing he knew for certain after tonight: he had to walk away. He would not allow her to be subjected to the kind of pressure her parents had exerted tonight. It wasn't fair to expect her to give up so much for a life with him. She ought to go back to Townsend and all the advantages she could have in Charleston.

He turned into the gate of the Hanford estate and drove to his parents' cottage without once looking in the direction of the main house. The cottage lights were still on, which meant his mother was probably up knitting while his father slept in an easy chair, a book open on his chest. He glanced in a window at the familiar scene and smiled. It gave him an odd sense of continuity.

He tapped on the door and heard his father's startled, "What's that?"

"I'll get it, John. Put your shoes on." His mother opened the door a crack and peeked out. "Paul!"

Her round, wrinkled face lit with pleasure and she enfolded him in plump arms. She smelled of talcum powder and a vague hint of cinnamon. She'd probably baked a coffee cake for the Hanfords' breakfast, he thought, recalling how Christine had loved it. As a child she'd often stolen a portion from the breakfast table for him, then they'd shared it as they sat side by side in the tree house his father had built for them in a giant oak.

His father was on his feet now, moving more slowly than he'd remembered. Years of kneeling on cold, damp ground had made his knees stiff. "Boy, what brings you out here at this hour on a weeknight? Everything okay?"

"Give him a minute to settle down," his mother chided. "Come into the kitchen. I've just baked a coffee cake. We'll have that and I'll make a fresh pot of coffee."

"What will the Hanfords do in the morning, if we eat their breakfast?" Paul asked.

"They'll get oatmeal. It's better for Mr. Hanford anyway," she said, giving him a conspiratorial grin.

Within minutes they were settled around the kitchen table as they had been a thousand times in the past. It was where family decisions were always made, amid good food and gentle love.

"Work going okay?" his father asked, probing carefully.

"Fine, Pop. I have more business than I can handle." He hesitated, then added, "I'm working with someone now."

"Oh?"

He began, then, to tell them about Gabrielle and Second Chances, about the jobs they'd done, about her talent and enthusiasm.

"She's more than a business partner, isn't she?" his mother asked with her incredible perceptiveness. "You're in love with her."

He grinned ruefully. "It's that plain?"

"It is to me. You don't come home talking about casual friends with that special gleam in your eyes. You haven't looked that way since..." She broke off uneasily.

"Since Christine. You can say it, Ma."

"You're better off without her. Surely you see that, son," his father said. "She'd have brought you nothing but misery. She was spoiled rotten by her daddy. Maybe that wasn't her fault, but it turned her into a user. She took from you without paying no mind to your feelings. She deserves that empty, cold marriage she's found herself in."

It was not the first time Paul had heard references to Christine's unhappiness, but he found that at last it meant nothing. He simply felt sorry for her, as he would for anyone trapped in an impossible situation of their own making.

"Are you going to marry this Gabrielle?" his mother asked.

"I don't think so, Ma. She's...she's a lot like Christine."

His mother gasped softly and frowned. His father looked just as worried. "Now, son, you're too old to be needing advice from me, but I've got to warn you—"

He held up his hand. "It's okay. You don't need to say it. I met her parents tonight and I think I finally realized why it wouldn't work. She'd be caught between us."

His mother stirred her coffee, her expression thoughtful. "Does that mean you think she's in love with you?"

"She says she is."

"But you said . . ."

"When I said she was like Christine, I didn't mean she was selfish. I just meant that she comes from the same kind of privileged background. Her father's Senator Graham Clayton, for God's sake. He could hand her the world on a platter."

His parents exchanged another worried glance. "But she's satisfied with what you can give her?" his mother asked quietly.

"She claims she is, but *I* can see it's not enough. She deserves all those things she can have if she goes back to South Carolina. Until tonight I'd been able to ignore the fact that I was denying her things that should rightfully be hers."

"If you walk out of her life, do you honestly think that's what she'll do? Will she go home?"

He stared at his mother and thought of Gabrielle's determination to make her own way, her absolute refusal to consider going back or even accepting help from home. It was a perspective he hadn't considered. "No. I don't suppose she would."

"Is she smart?"

He grinned at that. "A hell of a lot smarter than I am at times."

"Then she wouldn't do something dumb like staying with you, if she thought it was wrong for her, now would she?"

He laughed and suddenly the doubts began to dissipate. "I don't suppose she would."

"And she's smart enough to recognize a decent, caring man?"

He stood up, pulled his mother from her chair and swung her around. "Thanks, Ma."

He bent down and gave his father a kiss that left a startled but pleased look on his face. "If this works out, I want you to come to dinner with us on Sunday."

"No ifs. It will work out. You bring her here," his mother countered. "I'll make pot roast."

"No. I want you to sit back and enjoy a meal for a change. Besides, you haven't seen the apartment since we fixed it up." He grinned at his father. "And I think Gabrielle would love your ideas for the garden. It seems she aspires to a green thumb. She's got bulbs scattered all over the place and can't decide where to plant them. If we don't get them in the ground soon, I'm liable to cook them for dinner one night by mistake."

"If you want to make us really happy on Sunday, you'll announce your engagement. I'm ready for some grandbabies to take care of."

"I'll do my best, Ma."

He drove home with a silly, expectant grin on his face. He and Gabrielle were going to work this out. He would do his best to win over her parents, but he wasn't marrying them.

Marrying?

Well, hell, wasn't that what this was all about? He'd been half-crazy in love with the woman from the first minute she'd appeared on his doorstep with her fox coat, stubborn chin and vulnerable eyes. He admired her strength and honesty. He thrilled to her sharp wit. And he cherished her gentleness. The images that flashed through his mind now weren't of a sophisticated, stylishly dressed woman, but of Gabrielle with paint on the tips of her eyelashes, hands that smelled of turpentine and a smile that grew at the sight of him. Yes, marrying was definitely what this was all about. He was whistling when he went up the stairs at 2:00 a.m., the future as clear to him and as filled with promise as it could possibly be.

The only light on in the apartment was the Tiffany lamp in the kitchen. He found Gabrielle in her bed, her cheeks still damp with tears. Had they been for him or for the life she'd given up?

Filled with wonder by her beauty, he gazed down at the hair spread across the pillow like threads of gold. He traced the full curve of lips still pouty from the urgent kisses he'd stolen before her parents' arrival. Such a passionate, giving lover. He'd never imagined such ecstasy was possible, not for anyone, much less him.

But, despite the optimism he'd felt with his parents and on the long ride home, he wondered fleetingly if he was wrong. Could this really last? After the initial period of adjustment, he and Gabrielle had lived together in almost perfect harmony for these past weeks. But he'd always felt the arrangement was temporary.

It was as if she was simply on loan to him, as if she could be taken away at any instant and returned to her rightful place in the world.

Suddenly he wanted, no, *needed* a commitment. Until now Gabrielle had been the one in search of new goals and possibilities. He had encouraged the search, but done very little to assure his own place in her future. Tonight had changed that in some immeasurable way. The link between them, always unspoken, but always at the center of his thoughts, had to be forged now into something lasting. If he lost her after this, he knew with absolute certainty that he would never find a replacement to equal her.

He brushed her cheek with a gentle caress, then slipped from the bed. He needed movement to keep pace with his thoughts. He glanced into his own sparsely furnished room and wondered if he'd ever be able to sleep there alone again. He wandered through the living room, touching the tables she had refinished with such love, the sofa she had spent days cleaning until the fabric was almost as bright as new. He paused at the round oak table, still set for a dinner that had very nearly caused him to run from the one thing that would make his life complete: Gabrielle's love.

He touched the china, the crystal, the silver, the linen napkins. All bore the unmistakable mark of wealth and good taste. Yet Gabrielle had seemed perfectly content for all this time with cheap plates and stainless steel utensils. She had adapted to his life-style with an ease and willingness that astounded him now that he saw this new evidence of what she'd been used to. Even more remarkable was the fact that with the trappings of money so close at hand, she had never once imposed them on him. Until last night, when she had wanted to do something special for the all-important first meeting between him and her parents.

His own compromises had been far less. In fact he'd done nothing to change his way of life to accommodate hers. If anything, he had taken advantage of her loss of income as a way of keeping her his economic equal. Consciously or unconsciously, he had been testing Gabrielle, waiting for her to fail, waiting for the moment when she railed at their modest life-style and demanded more. It made him sick to think how unfair he'd been.

So, tell her, he thought, staring out the window. Expose your own vulnerabilities for a change. Ask her to get married and see if she'll run or stay. It was, of course, the ultimate test.

As he peered into the darkness, telling himself it might be too soon to talk about a lasting, forever kind of love, too risky to make plans for the future, he saw the first flakes of snow drifting down. For the first time in his life, he saw them not as the promise of back-breaking chores, but as a hint of magic and beauty that had to be shared.

He went back to the bedroom, sat on the edge of the bed and shook Gabrielle gently. "Wake up."

A smile played across her lips, but her eyes remained tightly shut.

"Gaby."

"Mmm."

"Wake up. I want to show you something."

"You're back," she murmured with quiet surprise.

"I'm back," he confirmed.

"I'm glad." Her hand, still warm from resting beneath her cheek, crept into his and clung. Then she sighed contentedly and closed her eyes again.

"Sweetheart, wake up."

"Is it morning?"

"No."

She blinked, tried to focus her gaze, then patted his cheek. "Go back to sleep."

He shook his head and grinned. He went back into the living room where he'd tossed his jacket across a chair. Then he came back and pushed open her window. He wrapped the covers securely around Gabrielle and scooped her up in his arms. She nuzzled against his neck, murmuring her contentment. The brush of her lips against his skin almost made him forget his goal. It would be very easy to climb back into bed with her and go about waking her in an entirely different way.

But tonight was about more than their bond of physical love. It deserved a special kind of magic. Holding her tightly, he stepped out onto the fire escape.

The blast of cold air snapped her awake at once. She stared around blankly, her gaze finally locking with his. "Paul, what are we doing on the fire escape in the dark?" She glanced down, her eyes widening. "When I'm only wearing a blanket?"

"You'll see," he promised evasively.

"Are you planning to throw me off the roof?" she inquired calmly as he began climbing up the fire escape.

He grinned. "Not unless you give me any problems."

She nodded, yawning sleepily and nuzzling closer. "Good."

When they were on the roof, he stared around at the scattered lights, the inky sky, then lifted his face for the soft touch of snowflakes melting against his skin. "Look up," he told Gabrielle.

She held her head back and gazed at the sky. When the first snowflake caressed her cheek, she touched the spot with an expression of dawning understanding. Her eyes sparkled with delight as the snow began to fall more heavily.

"It's snowing," she said softly, her tone filled with awe. "The first time this winter."

Paul shook his head, feeling a stirring of amazement and happiness deep in his chest. "It's moondust."

She grinned at the whimsical statement. "There's no moon."

"Of course not," he explained patiently. "It's inside, being chipped into millions of specks of moondust. It only happens on special occasions."

"Oh, really," she said, laughing. "Which occasions are those?"

His gaze met hers and the sparks began to blaze, sparks so hot they endangered the snow. "When two people fall in love."

She gasped softly and her eyes filled again with wonder. "Oh, Paul. It's going to be okay after all, isn't it?"

Her lips sought his, warm and pliant and moist from the kiss of the moondust. There was magic in the kiss, a spell that dared him to go on, the words whispering across her mouth. "Marry me, Gabrielle."

Her answer was in the soft moan of pleasure, the hungry demand of her lips on his, the teasing invasion of her tongue.

"Is that a yes?" he asked, breathing heavily.

"Yes."

"We'll have problems," he warned.

"Never."

He'd never heard a more unrealistic claim, but he loved her optimism. "We'll work them out," he corrected. "I may never be able to give you what you're used to. There won't be diamonds, just moondust."

"This," she said, curving her arms around his neck. "This is what I want to get used to. I was so afraid I'd lost you tonight. Do you have any idea how much you've given me, how empty my life would be without you?"

"I've given you?" he repeated incredulously.

"Of course. Hopes, dreams, belief in myself. Not to mention that I've never before been swept from my bed in the middle of the night to see the first snowfall."

"I should hope not."

"Don't make jokes. This is the most romantic proposal any woman could ever have. Our children will be awed and amazed that their practical, down-to-earth father did it.''

''Our children?'' he said weakly, thinking that his first cautious step was quickly turning into a race toward the future. He felt as though he'd put one tentative toe into an ocean and been caught up by the tide.

''They'll be beautiful,'' she promised, apparently captivated by the idea. ''They'll be smart and creative. Very creative.''

''Obedient?'' he asked hopefully, the prospect beginning to take on a certain appeal for him, as well. His mother would be ecstatic.

''Stubborn,'' she said ruefully.

''No doubt. At the risk of sounding like I'm rushing things, how soon do you plan on expanding our family?''

''Well, it does take time,'' she said with just a hint of regret. ''I can't just go to the store in the morning and pick out two or three.''

He chuckled. ''I do know where they come from.''

She touched his cheek. ''From nights like tonight.''

Emotion crowded his chest. Joy sang through his veins. He swallowed hard. ''God, I love you.''

''Show me, then. Take me inside and show me.''

Inside, with the magic of moondust swirling around them, they found that little corner of heaven where dreams become reality.

Paul awoke in the morning to the touch of something very cold against his lips. His eyes snapped open to find Gabrielle kneeling on the bed beside him, her hands filled with snow. He grinned. "If you're planning to do what I think you're planning to do, forget it. I'm bigger and stronger and I will get even."

"It's moondust, remember? I'm saving it."

"It will have a very short life expectancy curled up in your hand like that."

Her expression sobered. "Will our love melt the same way someday, Paul?"

He pulled her down beside him. "No. Not if we don't let it."

"But you almost left me for good last night, didn't you?"

"Almost," he admitted. "But not because of anything you did. Not even because I didn't believe in our love."

"My parents?"

"Yes. They threw me. I realized how much I was asking you to give up."

"It's my decision, Paul. Yours and mine. My parents will learn to live with whatever we decide."

"I told you last night, I'll never be able to match the life you've left. Our children won't be wearing designer diapers and going to fancy preschools that teach piano to two-year-olds. Can you really accept that?"

"Designer diapers? Piano lessons?" she repeated incredulously. "That's really what's been worrying you, isn't it?"

His silence was answer enough. She went on. "Darling, if what I grew up with was so irresistible, do you think I would have left it? The only thing important for a relationship and for kids is love and the commitment to do the very best we can. We have that.''

His hands caressed her cheeks as he searched her eyes. They were glowing with the truth of her love. "Then I guess there's just one thing left to do," he said.

"What's that?"

"Set a wedding date."

She threw herself into his arms. "I do love you," she said, dropping kisses over his face.

He swallowed hard, torn between laughter and desire. She tilted her head and stared at him. "This is a very serious moment in our lives, Paul Reed. What's so funny?"

"Your moondust is melting down my back."

An impish light flared in her eyes as she moved behind him. "We certainly won't want to lose any of that," she said seriously as her tongue set out to capture every drop.

"Umm, Gaby," Paul said as a shiver sped down his spine. "Do you think we might want to keep some of this moondust in the freezer? It may be hard to come by in August and I'm definitely beginning to see several interesting uses for it."

She tangled her bare legs with his and ran her hands provocatively down his chest. "We can always use our imaginations."

Paul closed his eyes and absorbed the wicked sensations. She was right, he thought before giving himself entirely over to her touches. The moondust would always be with them and, if treasured, like diamonds it would only increase in value with time.

*   *   *   *   *

SILHOUETTE® Desire®

ANOTHER BRIDE FOR A BRANIGAN BROTHER!

Branigan's Touch
by Leslie Davis Guccione

Available in October 1989

You've written in asking for more about the Branigan brothers, so we decided to give you Jody's story—from *his* perspective.

Look for Mr. October—*Branigan's Touch*—a *Man of the Month*, coming from Silhouette Desire.

Following #311 *Bittersweet Harvest*, #353 *Still Waters* and #376 *Something in Common*, *Branigan's Touch* still stands on its own. You'll enjoy the warmth and charm of the Branigan clan—and watch the sparks fly when another Branigan man meets his match with an O'Connor woman!

SD523-1